D1203298

Date: 5/24/22

GRA HIROTSUGU V.2
Hirotsugu, Ryusen,
She professed herself pupil
of the wise man.

PALM BEACH COUNTY
LIBRARY SYSTEM
3650 Summit Boulevard
West Palm Beach, FL 33406-4198

She Professed Herself Pupil of the Wise Man

NOVEL
2

WRITTEN BY

Ryusen
Hirotsugu

ILLUSTRATED BY

fuzichoco

Airship

Seven Seas Entertainment

TABLE OF CONTENTS

Kenja no deshi wo nanoru kenja 2
©Ryusen Hirotsugu (Story) ©fuzichoco (Illustrations)
This edition originally published in Japan in 2014 by
MICRO MAGAZINE, INC., Tokyo.
English translation rights arranged with
MICRO MAGAZINE, INC., Tokyo.

No portion of this book may be reproduced or transmitted
in any form without written permission from the copyright
holders. This is a work of fiction. Names, characters, places,
and incidents are the products of the author's imagination
or are used fictitiously. Any resemblance to actual events,
locales, or persons, living or dead, is entirely coincidental.
Any information or opinions expressed by the creators of this
book belong to those individual creators and do not necessarily
reflect the views of Seven Seas Entertainment or its employees.

Seven Seas press and purchase enquiries can be sent to
Marketing Manager Lianne Sentar at press@gomanga.com.
Information regarding the distribution and purchase of
digital editions is available from Digital Manager CK Russell
at digital@gomanga.com.

Seven Seas and the Seven Seas logo are trademarks of
Seven Seas Entertainment. All rights reserved.

Follow Seven Seas Entertainment online at
sevenseasentertainment.com.

TRANSLATION: Wesley O'Donnell
ADAPTATION: Adam Lee
COVER DESIGN: Nicky Lim
LOGO DESIGN: George Panella
INTERIOR LAYOUT & DESIGN: Clay Gardner
PROOFREADER: Meg van Huygen
LIGHT NOVEL EDITOR: T. Anne
PRINT MANAGER: Rhiannon Rasmussen-Silverstein
PRODUCTION MANAGER: Lissa Pattillo
MANAGING EDITOR: Julie Davis
ASSOCIATE PUBLISHER: Adam Arnold
PUBLISHER: Jason DeAngelis

ISBN: 978-1-64827-441-1
Printed in Canada
First Printing: November 2021
10 9 8 7 6 5 4 3 2 1

THE AFTERNOON seemed calculated to inspire optimism.

Birds wheeled through a cloudless sky, soaring aloft on invisible air currents. Below, the lush green top of a primal forest blanketed the landscape for as far as the eye could see. As the spring breeze blew through the forest, it carried the scent of new growth and life.

To those traveling the road beneath the dense canopy of leaves, breaks in the foliage shone like stars on a dark night, and pools of dappled sunlight fell on the forest floor around their feet. Occasionally, a sunbeam would shimmer like a meteor on a starlit night.

In the middle of the road was a gentleman in a military uniform standing alongside an adorable girl done up in gothic lolita chic. They stared at the side of their carriage, stunned looks on both their faces. A gentle breeze caressed Mira's cheek and sent her long silver hair fluttering. Her face began to turn pale as she took in the reddish-brown smear on the side of their carriage. Garrett stood with lips pursed, eyes fixed on what was lying on the ground.

The road was level and wide enough for two carriages to pass each other with room to spare. The visibility was good despite the dense nature of the surrounding forest.

Still...things like this occasionally happened.

With growing irritation, Mira forced herself to look at the form which lay before them. A rag-clad body sprawled motionless on the roadside. One of its arms had been torn off and sent flying, to land somewhere ahead of the coach. The rest of its limbs were in a tangle of impossible angles and dislocated joints.

A clear case of a body hit by a speeding vehicle.

"Well, you've really stepped in it now," Mira said gravely. She regretted not recommending that Garrett attend some sort of remedial driving school before they left the palace.

"J-just a moment, Miss Mira! He came out of nowhere! I didn't have time to stop!" Garrett fumbled for any excuse he could find.

It was true that the forest itself was so deep and dense that it could have easily concealed man or monster. But while the highway was dimly lit beneath the canopy, it wasn't nearly dark enough to miss someone walking along the roadside. Garrett should have been able to see clearly from his perch on the coachman's seat.

Mira let his excuses wash over her as she stared mutely at Garrett. For a moment, her eyes seemed to flicker with pity, and then she gave a small nod and walked down the road toward the severed arm. Garrett returned the nod and breathed a sigh of relief at having an ally, despite how bad the situation looked for him.

Accidents were accidents. The incident would have to be reported and there would be an investigation, of course. At least he had Mira in his corner. As he considered what to do about the corpse, his eyes drifted from the main part of the body over to the torn-off arm. And then a bit farther past that.

"Miss Mira, how far are you going?!" Garret called. He'd assumed she was heading over to collect the arm, but she'd gone well past it and showed no signs of turning back.

"I told you that I was leaving this mess to you, didn't I?"

"You said nothing of the sort!"

"I nodded. And you nodded back. Right?"

"That's what that meant?!"

It appeared that the pair weren't yet familiar enough to communicate via body language.

"What seems to be the problem?" An unfamiliar voice interrupted their bickering.

Turning, they saw a sturdy-looking man clad in metal armor. Behind him, a dozen or so meters back, sat a carriage that looked like it belonged to a merchant. As Garrett realized the interloper was a hired bodyguard, he looked up at the forest canopy with a humorless grin. He had no doubt that news of this accident would travel through the merchant's information network in the blink of an eye.

His goose was well and truly cooked.

As the shock of the accident and sudden encounter with other travelers wore off, Mira stared at the guard with a tight smile plastered to her face and hoped she wouldn't be implicated as well.

Taking in their expressions, the man frowned and looked down at the body by their feet. Then comprehension dawned and he locked his gaze back on Garrett.

"I see, we've been having trouble with this sort as well," he offered sympathetically before letting out a nasty chuckle.

The guard walked over and turned the corpse over with his boot. Underneath the body's rotting, bark-like robes, they could make out a skeleton of weathered bone smeared with rust-colored clay. Instead of skin and flesh, the body was composed of clumps of earth and dead vegetation. Not a drop of blood had been shed.

Garret blew out a massive sigh of relief, and Mira chuckled as though she'd never thought otherwise.

"It looks like a zombie, but they shouldn't be out at this time of the day." Garrett eyed the body on the ground with suspicion. While the forest road was shady, sunlight still flowed down past the outstretched leaves of the trees.

"Hrmm, indeed," Mira said, putting her finger to her chin and nodding as she walked over to a sunbeam breaking through the canopy.

"You two must be new around here. Otherwise, you'd already know." The guard's gaze switched back and forth between Mira, Garrett, and the carriage. "These weirdos started showing up about a month ago. They're weak and harmless...so far. But we don't know what's been causing them, so better safe than sorry."

The guard went on to explain some of the recent events that had been plaguing the local area. Zombies roamed freely at night, but oddly enough, there were no accounts of any attacks on humans. Still, they damaged crops and fields as they trampled across the countryside.

During daylight hours, they'd lurk in darker areas of the forest. Other travelers along the road had similar accidents to report.

"Anyway, the local government formed hunting parties to clear them out a couple weeks ago," the guard said with a sigh before knitting his brow in distaste. "The pay was good, so I joined up. But...they don't put up any resistance. It was really unsettling."

He glanced down at the zombie lying on the road and gave it another light prod with his boot. "They don't attack people; they don't fight back. I wonder what they're after?"

"It's definitely out of the ordinary," Mira muttered to herself as she and Garrett joined in staring at the strange corpse.

For even a novice adventurer, it was common knowledge that undead monsters such as zombies wouldn't appear until after the sun had fully set. Outside of a dungeon that never saw the light of day, those monsters were only seen during the night.

"Nobody seems to know what they are or where they came from," said the guard as he helped Garrett move the corpse to the side of the road.

With that chore complete, he bid them a fair journey. The two continued on their way, hoping to banish the whole creepy incident from their memory.

As the summoner known formerly as Danblf, one of the Nine Wise Men of Alcait, Mira had a wealth of knowledge when it came to the rules of *Ark Earth Online*. None of them squared with what the guard said, or what she had seen lying on the ground at her feet.

This development was an unwelcome distraction from her mission to search and locate seven of her former comrades and compel them to return and defend their kingdom.

Three days had passed since they left the capital at Lunatic Lake. Mira was still getting used to traveling by coach, but found that she greatly enjoyed the local cuisine when they stopped at taverns and waystations along their route. Each kilometer they traveled brought them closer to her destination—the C-Rank dungeon called the Ancient Temple Nebrapolis.

As the western sky began to turn the deep scarlet of dusk, they passed through the main gates of Karanak, the City of Requiem. In the main square stood a stone monument dedicated to praying for the peaceful repose of heroic spirits who served in wars long past. While there were many dungeons in the surrounding area that brought adventurers to the city, it was surprisingly quiet this evening. It seemed almost gloomy, even.

Mira was idly gazing at the few forms moving about the sparsely populated street when she tumbled out of her seat. The carriage had suddenly drawn to a halt.

"Good grief, Garrett! What now?" Puckering her lips, she glared out the window.

Just past the horses, she caught sight of Garrett's bowed head as he looked at something in the street. A body was sprawled on the avenue before the carriage.

Not again! Her eyes widened and her cheeks twitched.

"I'm terribly sorry, are you hurt?" Garrett offered a hand and the body lying on the ground slowly began to move.

"Oh, no, that was my fault for just jumping out like that." The old man lying on the cobblestones looked up and accepted the vice captain's proffered hand, using it to pull himself to his feet.

Despite not having a hair on his head, he seemed to be in surprisingly good health for a man of his years—in fact, his physique was on par with someone half his age. It seemed that he'd been distracted and failed to notice their carriage until he'd already stepped into the road.

Thankfully, the hooves of the horses came nowhere near him, and he appeared to be in good health. As Mira looked him over with a sense of relief, it occurred to her that he'd probably have been fine in any case, given his level of fitness.

"You seemed to be in quite the hurry; is everything all right?"

"My grandson hasn't come home yet, so I'm out looking for him. You know how strange the nights have been lately."

"Huh...? Oh! You mean the zombies we've been hearing about?"

"Yep, them's the ones. That's why I told him to be home before the sun sets. It's got us all spooked." His voice carried a twinge of sadness. "No casualties yet, but I suppose it's still worrisome."

That matched the story Mira and Garrett had heard from the guard. But just because the zombies hadn't attacked anyone *yet*, it didn't do much to quell the anxieties of parents and guardians. After a bit more chitchat, the old man apologized again and headed off toward the child's usual haunts with a parting bow.

"I thought the city felt a bit melancholy. Normally, the kids would be out playing before dinner," Mira said as she glanced about the quieter-than-normal city streets.

"They must've been told to be home before sundown." Garrett had returned to his position on the driver's stand. He scanned the area before flicking the reins.

He paused when his eyes passed over Mira and was struck with a sense of irony. She was a cute child—anyone would call her adorable—and yet he didn't feel the slightest concern about her walking about the city streets at night.

A few minutes later, the sound of the horses' hooves striking the street echoed softly as the coach entered the driveway of a large, three-story hotel. A little farther on was a wooden carriage house, where Garrett pulled into one of the stalls. As he stopped, the stable manager stepped up to take the reins.

"Welcome. Will you be staying with us tonight?"

"Indeed, we will."

"Very good, sir. We'll take care of your horses while you get settled in."

As Garrett offered his thanks, the stableman filled out a claim check and passed the slip of paper to the vice commander before taking a step back and bowing.

"Well, Miss Mira, I suppose we should go check in. Shall we?" Garrett gracefully leapt down from the driver's stand and swiftly had the carriage door open before Mira had even risen from her seat.

"Sure," she replied, studiously ignoring his flourish as she stepped out of the coach.

Together they walked in the direction of the lobby, passing a large chunk of marble situated next to the entrance. The slab was adorned with a lantern, and the name of the establishment was carved ornately into the stone.

Garrett opened the door, ushering Mira into a lobby that would put most high-class hotels to shame. At the front desk, uniformed employees took care of the guests' needs in a quick and calm manner. The main window looked out on an enclosed garden, where children ran about between neatly pruned trees and flower beds in the twilight.

But a group of adventurers dressed in fine armor and robes seated in the chairs by the window lent an otherworldly atmosphere to the scene. The blend of Western-style hotel architecture with sword-and-sorcery patrons was slightly jarring.

"Well, now, isn't this lovely?" murmured Mira as she took it all in.

It wasn't quite as fancy as the palace in Alcait, but the state of cleanliness, the conduct of the staff, and the casually elegant décor wasn't far off from the accommodations at Lunatic Lake.

"This is the finest hotel in Karanak," said Garrett in a soft voice as he watched her gaze around the lobby. "We'd have to go to the capital to find a finer establishment."

"Sounds expensive... I don't have all that much on me." Mira put a hand to the black pouch at her waist and furrowed her brow. The waist pouch had come from the bag given to her by the palace maids, and it perfectly accented her two-toned outfit. Inside was the sack of coins that she'd received as a reward for defeating the

Lesser Demon—the sum total of all her cash, since her prodigious savings vanished when the game became real.

"Fret not, Miss Mira. King Solomon is covering our expenses on this journey." Garrett grinned before murmuring quietly to himself, "I've always wanted to stay here."

"You're unbelievable." Her tone was exasperated, but Mira couldn't help but smile as well.

While Garrett took care of checking them in, Mira wandered the lobby and looked about at the furniture and paintings that decorated the space—completely unaware that as she admired the furnishings, others were making their own secretive observations of her. This was a top-flight hotel, and it served high-ranked adventurers who were experts at making sure their attention went unnoticed.

With the formalities completed, an employee led her to her room. All of the best suites were occupied for the evening, but they still managed to find a room for her that would have been considered the crème de la crème at any ordinary inn. Nevertheless, she wistfully recalled her quarters in the tower of Evocation and wished she'd had more of a chance to enjoy her own bedroom. She consoled herself by thinking of Garrett, who was staying on the lower floor in one of the standard rooms.

As Mira explored her quarters, she found a note had been placed on the table. Opening it, she found details regarding the various services offered by the hotel. She could ring a bell by the door to summon room service, and she was invited to take meals during scheduled times in the hotel's dining hall. The note also informed her that she could check her room key with the front desk when she departed in the morning and she could pick it back up upon her return.

After skimming through the note, Mira turned to the large grandfather clock in the room. It was almost six in the evening. The sky outside her window was nearly pitch-black with just a faint vermilion glow far on the western horizon.

Hrmm, time to relax, I think. I'll get back to the grind tomorrow.

With an exhausted sigh, Mira withdrew a drink from her inventory and flopped down onto an overstuffed sofa. Several days of travel by carriage had left her drained, and the luxuries offered by a high-class hotel sounded like the cure to her troubles. She flipped open the room service menu and rang the bell without even glancing at the prices.

The next morning, she entered the dining hall and found Garrett, who had just finished enjoying his post-breakfast coffee.

"Good morning, Miss Mira!"

"Hrmm, morning." She nodded in greeting as she looked over the breakfast menu before her. Then her head shot up as a thought struck her.

There had been a lockbox secured in the carriage, and she had no idea what was in it.

"By the way, what are you doing after this?" She eyed Garrett suspiciously. "I'm sure you didn't come all this way just to escort me."

"You are correct, Miss Mira." Garrett lightly waved a sealed letter in his hand. "I have other matters to attend to at Fort Karanak."

"Oho, is it about that box that shared a seat with me?"

"Just so. It's a formal missive, if you will..." Garrett looked around the room and chose his words carefully. "Regarding the little *incident* we were tasked with a few days ago. The box contains a summary of alerts, joint-defense information, and orders for future measures."

"Hrmm, I see."

The *incident* in question was the attack on Alcait by a number of Lesser Demons. Mira had been wondering what the fiends' end goal was but had decided to leave that riddle to Solomon. She had her own fish to fry at the moment. Speaking of which...

"By the way, would you know where the Mages' Guild is?"

Garrett thought for a moment. "Let's see. To get to the Mages' Guild, take a left out of the hotel and just head straight for a little while."

"Hrmm, left and straight ahead, got it." Mira repeated the directions to herself to ensure she had them down.

"If you get lost on the way back, you can ask the Knight Patrol—they're in the white-and-blue armor—where the best hotel in town is and they'll tell you how to get back."

"That won't be necessary," Mira said with a huff before turning her menu toward Garrett and pointing at the *Croque Monsieur*.

"Ahh, Madam wishes to have the *Croque Monsieur*. Very good. And to drink?"

"Let's do the, uh...banana au lait."

"Of course," Garrett replied with a bemused smile. He rose from his seat and walked over to the counter to place Mira's order. Upon his return, he said cheerfully, "Now then, Miss Mira, I shall see you again this evening."

"Right, take care out there."

"I will. And I hope you'll make sure not to get lost," he added hastily before fleeing the dining hall.

"Hmph! I'm not going to get myself lost," Mira grumped as she glared at his turned back.

Twenty minutes later, full and having completely enjoyed her breakfast, Mira made her way toward the Mages' Guild.

**She
Professed
Herself
Pupil of the
Wise Man**

2

MIRA CREPT ALONG the edge of the street as she tried her best to remain inconspicuous. The morning rush was just calming down, but the main boulevard was so busy that Mira thought she'd merely imagined the gloomy scene from the night before. Many people easily recognizable as fighters or mages were among the crowds of people coming and going.

"Hrmm, is this the place?"

Just as Garrett had said, she came across two large stone buildings standing side by side not far from the entrance to the hotel. Signs hung above the respective doors, announcing that the left was the Fighters' Guild and the right was the Mages' Guild.

Double-checking the sign for the Mages' Guild, Mira reached for the door handle just as a loud voice rang out from the Fighters' Guild next door.

"Please help me! I've heard tales of your strength! You have to help me!"

The door to the Fighters' Guild flew open and a young boy—perhaps just ten years old—tumbled through as though he'd been tossed out. He tried to force his way back in but was blocked by a strong-looking man in metal armor with a troubled look on his face. As the kid clung to him, the fighter tried to push the boy back into the street.

"Look, kid, we'd like to help you...but the strongest people around here are D-Rank adventurers. It'd be suicide."

The boy refused to back down. Despite how the other adventurers leaving the building tried to calm him, he kept trying to push his way back through the door. Realizing that her first impression of child abuse was clearly a mistake, Mira decided to mind her own business and entered the Mages' Guild.

The guild building was well organized, with a line of counters facing the main area. Off to the side was a large bulletin board, and chairs were arranged around the lobby as a waiting area. At first glance, it could almost be mistaken for a city ward office! The real difference was in the clientele.

As it was the Mages' Guild, most of the people present were magic users of one sort or another. Most of them were wearing robes, but there was a small group who caused Mira to do a double take.

"Is this...*normal*?" she muttered as she gazed at the outfits worn by a contingent of young ladies who must have been around fifteen to sixteen years old. No two ways about it, they looked like stereotypical magical girls.

She'd been embarrassed enough by her own gothic lolita ensemble, absolutely certain that it caused her to stick out like a sore thumb. But now it appeared that she was in good company—or at least *similar* company. The idea that she wasn't alone in her fashion sensibilities (voluntary or otherwise) began to take shape. Her clothes were neither outlandish nor unique.

With a sudden rush of relief and a smile born of her inner liberation, Mira headed toward the reception counters. Each desk bore a different label, and among them was one labeled *New Registrants*.

"I'd like to register with the Guild. Is that an option at the moment?" Mira asked, feeling just like she was back at the DMV.

"Of course, I can help you with that. You'll be registering as a new applicant, I presume?" The receptionist assisting her was a professional-looking woman with long, blonde hair done up in a ponytail and held in place with a ribbon. She smiled cheerfully, and the nametag around her neck read *Eurica*.

"Correct." Mira relaxed upon seeing Eurica's welcoming smile. It was reassuring to know that her attire was entirely appropriate for her occupation.

"Very well. If you could fill this out, please."

As Mira looked at the documents presented to her, she reached into her pouch, retrieved an envelope, and placed it atop the pile. "I also have a letter of recommendation."

"A recommendation? Absolutely. I'll take that for you." Accepting the envelope, Eurica flipped it over and froze as she saw the seal.

New applicants coming in with letters of recommendation weren't common, but they were far from rare. A noble might have their private forces registered with the guild so that they could be sent to a dungeon in search of treasure—or perhaps a high-ranking adventurer might sponsor a promising newcomer. Eurica had handled applicants with letters of recommendation on many occasions.

But this was unprecedented.

Obviously, the girl standing before her was a mage since she was applying at the Mages' Guild. And sure, she might appear a bit willowy at first glance—but body size didn't mean much when it came to latent magical ability. Magical power wasn't overt like weapons and armor.

Eurica had assumed that the girl had met some high-ranked adventurer or aristocrat who had recognized her skills and offered her a recommendation. Based on her adorable appearance, she might even be some noble's daughter and was flipping the letter down to drop the family name. But the letter's seal was from neither a noble family nor a high-ranked adventurer.

The girl's reference was Solomon. King Solomon. Ruler of the Kingdom of Alcait.

"Ah..." The smile vanished from her face. This wasn't a decision she could make on her own, and she knew the guild leader needed to be notified of this at once. As she disappeared to the back of the office, she said, "S-so sorry. Just a moment, please!"

Mira stood at the counter with a perplexed look on her face and tried to imagine what the problem might be. Unable to come up with anything, she reached across the desk to pick up a pen and filled out the application paperwork. Then she turned to observe the interior of the Mages' Guild and the people who were there that morning.

A few minutes later, Eurica returned to the desk with her composure and smile regained once more. "My deepest apologies; thank you so much for waiting."

"I've completed the forms. Does this look right?" Mira pushed the papers across the desk and Eurica nodded as she checked them over.

"Yes, this all looks in order. Thank you. But about your letter of recommendation... Would you accompany me to the guild leader's office, please?"

"Hrmm, fine by me." Mira knew the letter was legitimate but wasn't surprised that it had put her on the management's radar. To her, Solomon was just a friend, but questions were bound to be asked when she claimed that she had the confidence of the king of Alcait.

Eurica signaled another nearby staff member to attend to her duties at the reception desk, then led Mira off to the third floor of the guild hall. Before a set of particularly ornate doors, she stopped and knocked.

"Come in," called a stern, elderly voice from inside.

"Excuse me, sir. The applicant is here to see you." Eurica bowed as she entered the room.

The office was tastefully decorated and had a subdued feel to it. The modest furnishings added gentle hints of color, and the wall behind the desk was dominated by a large bookshelf filled with a wide variety of tomes and documents—all neatly filed and organized. The gentleman occupying said desk stood and gave a subtle yet respectful bow.

"Thank you for your time, miss. I am Leoneil, leader of Mages' Guild here in Karanak." He seemed in relatively good condition for a man of his age. The crow's feet at the corners of his sharp eyes made it no secret that he'd spent many hours squinting at paperwork. He stepped over to a small reception area with a couple of chairs and a table laden with snacks and tea, beckoning for the young girl to join him.

"I'm Mira," came her usual curt introduction as she flopped down into a seat and sized up the cakes arrayed before her.

"Ah, Miss Mira, is it?" Leoneil took the documents from Eurica, giving them a cursory glance. "And would you happen to be the pupil of Master Danblf I've heard whispers about?"

From the look on his face, he already knew the answer.

As the head of the Mages' Guild, he received reports from all over the kingdom. Years of collecting information as a hobby had led him to organize his own intelligence agency, and one of the recent tidbits that had filtered through his network was the rumor that a pupil of the great summoner had made herself known. Reports also said the young, beautiful, silver-haired girl was a skilled summoner in her own right. And now it seemed the object of those rumors had found her way into his office.

"Indeed. News spreads fast," Mira said, gazing longingly at a tray of *petit fours*.

"That it does. The letter from King Solomon was confirmation enough." A slight trace of a satisfied smile played across his face as he rose and returned to his desk. Then he stamped Mira's application as *Approved*. "Normally, we would administer a test to ensure an applicant was up to the task of a C-Rank adventurer's duties. But when the king of Alcait endorses you as the pupil of Danblf himself...well, I believe we can skip the formalities."

"Um, um, excuse me! When you say Master Danblf, you mean *the* Master Danblf?!" she interjected. She knew it was rude to interrupt but couldn't stop the question from spilling out as she stood and looked back and forth from Mira to Leoneil with wide eyes.

"That's correct. *That* Master Danblf. Originator of refining techniques, founding hero of the kingdom, the One-Man Army, et cetera. That's the one." Leoneil chuckled at her reaction.

He had the benefit of his intelligence network for some advance warning, but Eurica knew that the Wise Man Danblf had been missing for thirty years. For someone claiming to be his pupil to casually stroll up to her registration desk, only to have the guild leader stamp her approval with hardly a second thought, was simply unprecedented. It was almost too much to take in.

Eurica's expression slowly filled with glee as she stared at Mira.

Leoneil stepped between the two ladies, breaking Eurica's gaze and clearing his throat, "Ahem...If you could see that these are filed properly?"

"O-of course, sir! Leave it to me!" she said just a little too loudly, taking the documents carefully with both hands while peeking around her boss at Mira before scampering off with the paperwork.

"Now, then, the official business is taken care of. You can head home if you'd like, but perhaps you'd indulge an old man with some conversation?" Leoneil's desire for knowledge thirsted for whatever might be known about Danblf's current situation and whereabouts. To have his professed pupil in his office was a rare opportunity.

"Hrmm. Fine by me." Mira figured it wouldn't hurt to have a friendly relationship with the leader of the Mages' Guild. That sort of bond could pay dividends in the future. Besides, she'd get to sample the confections and pastries laid out on his coffee table.

They spent a chunk of the morning chatting about this and that. In between bites of cake and sips of tea, her responses were matter-of-fact, and she did her best to make sure her cover story lined up with what she'd told Mariana and Lythalia, the aides in the Linked Silver Towers. She reiterated that Danblf had been in the Mystic City of Beasts but she was unaware if he was still there, and she wielded a Dark Knight summon of the same rank as her master, and so on.

Watching her apparent enjoyment with the snacks, Leoneil offered her more and she immediately nodded her assent.

"Now perhaps I can ask you a question of my own." Mira put down her empty teacup and fixed Leoneil with an expectant look.

"Well, of course," Leoneil responded with a raised eyebrow. "As much as I can answer."

"What can you tell me about the recent zombie disturbances?"

The situation had Mira more worried than she would care to admit. It was quite unlike anything that happened back in the game world, and she was on the edge of her seat as she awaited his reply.

"Hmm, you want to know what's causing this, do you? Well... so do I. We don't usually have undead monsters wandering around the area—the closest place to find undead is the Ancient Temple Nebrapolis. And we'd never seen ones made of earth and vegetation before this incident began."

Leoneil stood and retrieved a bundle of papers from his desk. He pulled out one sheet in particular and laid it out on the table. It was a listing of the characteristics of the zombies.

They wandered at night but didn't attack people. Their bodies comprised earth and decaying plant material. They lurked in the shadows during the day and avoided the sunlight, but they would occasionally emerge in the shadows of the forest to be hit by carriages.

There were a few instances of them collapsing in front of houses after they were too late to escape the sunlight—but there were no recorded incidents of violence.

Their motives? Unknown.

Their origin? Unknown.

Their threat level? Unknown.

Whether or not they could *even be* classified as monsters? Unknown.

Mira made a dissatisfied face as she read through the report.

"I'm not being secretive; as you can see, we simply don't know." Leoneil turned and looked out his office window. Despite the concerning situation, there was a sparkle in his eye like a person who'd just spotted a clue in a detective novel. "I have my theories, but...I'd like to make arrangements to have the Ancient Temple investigated sometime soon."

"Oho, really now? Well, that's perfect. I've come to visit the temple myself. Perhaps I could provide a preliminary inspection of the area for you."

"That explains your need for the C-Rank license. Very well, then. I'd be obliged to have your assistance."

"But of course," Mira replied confidently as she popped the last bit of cake in her mouth. "Thanks for the snack. Until next time."

"I put a rush job on your registration. Your adventurer's license will be ready tomorrow morning."

With another quick thanks for the registration assistance, Mira patted her belly as she left the guild leader's office.

After the door closed, Leoneil picked up the recommendation letter from King Solomon and ruminated on it as he sat back heavily in his chair. She professed to be the pupil of Danblf. She had the backing of King Solomon. And she'd brashly declared that she was heading into the Ancient Temple.

He was certain there was an unseen current flowing beneath all of this, but he couldn't sense any malice or ill intent in the girl's demeanor. From the way she dug into the cake, leaving frosting smeared on her cheek, she was just an ordinary little girl—but occasionally, her gestures and choice of words deviated from that appearance.

Leoneil read the letter again, and a line caught his eye. He sank deeper into his chair. It was a request from King Solomon to issue Mira a pass to enter the forbidden Primal Forest. A point she hadn't mentioned at all during their chat.

CHAPTER 2

"Hmm. How strange, indeed."

Tossing the letter onto his desk, he looked out at the sky.

She Professed Herself Pupil of the Wise Man

3

WITH HER INTERACTION with the local bureaucracy concluded, Mira sat and watched adventurers pass by on the main street.

Mixed in with the traditional adventuring looks of armor and robes were some truly outrageous appearances, even by the standards of her own magical-girl attire. American-style ninjas made no effort to conceal themselves. Samurai passed by, strapped with numerous blades. There were even nuns wearing traditional demon masks, and no one seemed to react as if anything were amiss.

Maybe I don't stand out that much after all, she thought to herself as she glanced down at her own outfit. With all that on parade, it didn't seem she had much to worry about—so long as she ignored the fact that her physical appearance garnered more attention than her clothing.

She'd expected the process at the guild to take quite a bit longer. Now it was just past noon, and Mira was at a loss for what to do with the rest of her day. Her license wouldn't be ready until tomorrow morning, so she had some time to kill.

A woman—specifically an adventurer, wearing a robe with a thigh slit cut all the way to her hip—passed before her and entered a nearby item shop. Mira's gaze followed to the shop window, which was lined with all sorts of unfamiliar adventuring equipment entirely. Her eyes gleamed with curiosity.

Hrmm! Perhaps some investigating is in order...

Deciding that a bit of retail therapy might be a way to amuse herself while coming to terms with this new world, Mira bounced into the item shop.

She gazed in wonder at the items on display, and the differences between the game and her new reality began to dawn on her. Before, the items found in these shops were just used as decoration or to assist in battle—but now they had practical applications in everyday life, like cooking and lighting.

How interesting. Mira smirked to herself as she played with the direction of the wind on what appeared to be a fan-like apparatus that sucked air in on one side and blew out it out the other. The tantalizing slitted robe from earlier fluttered in the path of the current, and Mira drew a disapproving look from its owner.

Mira made her way from shop to shop—everything from armories to apothecaries—and with each passing store, her eyes sparkled. But as she exited the eleventh shop, she saw a gathering crowd and drew to a stop.

In her wandering, she'd strayed from the main road. The crowd in question murmured and shuffled a bit deeper inside a neighboring residential area.

Wonder what's got them all in a tizzy?

Thinking of it as her own instinctive curiosity, rather than crass rubbernecking, she found herself drawn into the crowd. Using her small body, she slipped through the gaps and made her way to the source of the commotion. At first glance, it was just an ordinary wooden house. Wilted flowers sprouted from neglected planters lining the windowsills, but that wasn't what had attracted all this attention.

A zombie sat propped up in the shadow of the doorway. A tattered bit of burnt and torn leather—possibly the remnant of a jacket—was stuck to the zombie's shoulder.

A nearby patrolman uttered a warning to the crowd. "Please stay back! This is the scene of an active investigation and may be dangerous!" His enameled white-and-blue armor marked him as a member of the Knight Patrol.

Administered by the Royal Alcait Military Police, the Knight Patrol served as the local police force for cities within the kingdom's borders. The Alcaitian coat of arms was engraved prominently on the armor that served as their uniform.

At the moment, two officers were present, one holding back the onlookers while the other stood with his hand on his sword hilt and warily watched the motionless zombie.

What's it doing out at this hour? Mira wondered. *The sun's still high in the sky.*

The noonday sun hung directly overhead, casting barely the slimmest shadows. Mira looked up and squinted at the glare before returning her gaze to the zombie. As the crowd watched, the puddle of shadow it had been sheltering in slowly vanished.

"Something's not right here," muttered the officer as he unclasped his scabbard and poked the monster's shoulder with it. A whisper broke out and spread among the crowd.

There was no sign of response from the zombie. The knight reached out and poked it again, this time more forcefully. The zombie jolted. Quiet enveloped the crowd once more.

As they looked on with bated breath, the zombie slowly tilted to one side before toppling to the ground. The limbs collapsed into small piles of dust as the two guards exchanged bitter smiles.

"Move along, folks. Just a false alarm!" called the officer serving as crowd control.

As the crowd dispersed and splintered into smaller groups, rumors of what happened started to spread through the town.

Hrmm. So this one was made up of earth and vegetation too, Mira thought to herself as she watched the guards stand over the remains. *Seeing it under proper light like this, it's almost more of a necromantic golem than a zombie.*

Mira knew a little about necromancy. The technique to create a necromantic golem typically imbued a dead body or inorganic matter with a temporary soul created by the magician. In the hands of a skilled necromancer, bodies revived by this technique were even able to temporarily use the abilities they had while still alive. And since they possessed a soul—unlike undead monsters— they could withstand the light of the sun.

Though from what I've heard, they still try to avoid daylight. Perhaps it's something else, she thought. *It's similar to a golem construct, but...it's more like a skeleton wearing a golem costume. Perhaps some new technique?*

It truly was a riddle.

As Mira pondered, another member of the Knight Patrol arrived, carrying a large box. Gathering up the scattered remains of the zombie, the officers packed them away to be taken to an evidence locker.

"What's this, a ring?" one called. "I hope it's not cursed."

The knight scowled as he picked up a simple golden ring from the remains before quickly tossing it into the box.

Watching the proceedings, Mira couldn't help but think of her friend and target. She wondered if Soul Howl was tied up in all of this. He'd always been a bit strange, but his knowledge and skills when it came to necromancy were second to none. She made a mental note to press the issue when she located him.

Their job complete, the Knight Patrol moved out. The crowd had dispersed, and order had been restored to the street. With nothing more to see, Mira turned back toward the main street, thinking there was still time to browse a few more shops.

"Huh?! There's nothing here!" A worried yell cut through the silence.

Farther down the street stood an elven woman with long black hair. Clad in white-and-green light armor, she had a thin sword attached to her hip and a gentle expression in her eyes. She glanced about as though searching for something.

As she walked past, Mira figured she must just be another onlooker who'd come to gawk at the zombie. But in the same instant, the woman spun around and her eyes landed on Mira.

"Ah! A moment please, miss!" The elf jogged over to Mira and then leaned forward to peer into her eyes. She had a kind smile tempered by a hint of anxiety. "I'd heard a zombie had appeared in this area; do you know anything about that?"

Mira decided it was best just to skip to the end of the story. "Yeah, the guards just finished cleaning it up."

She broke eye contact with the woman and turned to point in the direction the Knight Patrol had gone. The remains of the zombie had been removed well enough that any newcomer to the scene would never even know it had been there.

"I see, I see. So, it's all been handled. Thank goodness. Thank you!"

The elven woman seemed to relax before she turned and knocked on the door the zombie had been leaning against. Letting her curiosity get the better of her, Mira stepped slightly closer to snoop into the lady's business.

"Ah, Miss Emella. What brings you here?" asked a simple, some-what demure-looking woman who emerged from the house. Her voice was soft but expressionless, and she tilted her head to the side.

"I'd heard a zombie appeared in the neighborhood and was worried. Are you all right?" asked the elven woman, apparently named Emella. She looked worried and reached forward to catch and squeeze the other woman's hand.

Zombie in the neighborhood?! More like on her doorstep! Mira amended the statement silently.

"Really now? I hadn't noticed," the woman replied as if it didn't concern her at all. Her face remained vacant.

"I see. I guess it wasn't a big issue after all," Emella said. "Thank goodness. But if you need anything, you let me know, all right?"

"I will. Thank you." After a quick goodbye, the woman closed the door.

Turning away from the house, Emella had a look of relief. For a moment, their eyes met, and Emella smiled softly as Mira pointed down at the doorstep beneath her feet.

"It was actually right where you're standing."

"Wha?!" Emella shrieked and leapt into the air before turning and casting a cautious look at where she'd just been.

"So you know the person who lives here?" Mira asked with a smirk as she gave a pointed look back toward the house.

Emella nodded with a slight pout. "I do. She's married to one of my former guildmates. We met through him and became friends."

"Former guildmate, huh?" Feeling the mood change, Mira dropped her smug expression. "I take it that he isn't with your guild anymore?"

Emella gazed at her friend's home, then dropped her head and nodded. A soft, sad smile crept over her face.

"Yeah. Our guild focuses on adventuring, and we regularly travel from city to city. It doesn't really provide stability."

"I can see how that might not be compatible with married life." Mira knew that the life of an adventurer was one of risk and chances—not exactly the best for someone with a home life or children.

"Right. So he—Thomas—took the exam to become a guild official here in the city. Thanks to the appreciation for his work

in our guild, he was accepted. He'd just started working when..."
She trailed off and her expression clouded over as she took a
quick peek back at the house.

"Did something happen?" Mira thought back to the counte-
nance of the woman she'd just seen at the door. Any hint at the
happiness of her married life had been thoroughly scrubbed away.

"A month ago, Thomas went to check the barrier around a
dungeon and never came back. A search party was sent out, but
they couldn't find him. Even our private guild went looking for
him. We couldn't find a single clue."

As she spoke, Emella's tone sounded like she was venting her
own feelings of inadequacy and a frustration that they couldn't
do more to help. After looking sullen for a few moments, she
suddenly looked up and her expression flipped.

"Anyway, sorry about all that doom and gloom. But I'm sure
he's fine!" Emella beamed, but Mira could tell her words were
intended to reassure herself. "Thomas is the kind of person who
gets caught up in things and just vanishes; I'm sure he'll be back
before we know it. Well, then, see you around!"

With a casual salute, she turned and dashed off down the road.

She just bounces from one mood to another, Mira thought as
she watched Emella depart.

Then her gaze shifted, and her expression grew somber. This
house should have been filled with the joy and happiness of mar-
riage. Instead, even as it sat under the brilliant midday sun, it
exuded nothing but despair.

THE MORNING after registering with the Mages' Guild, Mira had a crisis on her hands.

She found herself sitting on her bed with the top half of her body exposed, trying and failing to figure out how to put on her bra. Lily, her attendant at the palace, had fitted her for the diabolical piece of clothing and clipped it onto her small frame with no trouble at all. Mira, on the other hand, was at a loss to understand how the accursed thing worked. She'd been ready to get her day started and was irritated that a piece of lingerie was proving to be the fiercest opponent she'd faced since arriving back in Alcait.

"Well, this just doesn't make any sense!" she exclaimed after struggling with the article of clothing for a while.

Finally, she gave up. The maidservants had warned of chafing and pain if she failed to wear the garment—but this was clearly an unwinnable battle. Mira flung the bra onto her bed before pulling her sleeveless top over her head in defeat.

She still emerged from her suite in time to have breakfast

with Garrett. His business at Fort Karanak was complete, but as evidenced by the small package he carried, he had other duties to attend to for the day. Mira sipped at her banana au lait as her thoughts drifted back to her own mission.

Commonly known as the catacombs, the Ancient Temple Nebrapolis comprised six levels that progressed deeper and deeper beneath the surface. It had been carved out of a rocky hillside and made for an impressive sight. Large stone statues of gods were carved on the slope. If not for the monsters, it would likely have been a thriving tourist destination.

But as the name implied, the catacombs were swarming with undead monsters. And it was that fact that made it irresistible to a mage like Soul Howl. One of the Nine Wise Men—and self-professed enthusiast of living-dead girls—he was the object of Mira's current hunt.

Finishing off the last of her drink, Mira sighed and donned her coat before strolling out onto the main street.

Arriving at the Mages' Guild, she noticed a familiar face. Eurica was hard at work filing paperwork this morning, instead of minding a counter. Despite their limited interaction, Mira still found it easier to approach her rather than engage with a complete stranger.

"Do you have a moment?" Mira asked. Eurica began to put aside the stack of papers she'd been working on.

"Of course, I'll be right with you." Then Eurica's eyes went wide. "Oh... Oh! Miss Mira, good morning! Ah, you're here for your adventurer's license, aren't you?"

"Indeed, is it ready?" Mira asked, boggling at how quickly Eurica could regain her professional composure.

"Yes, yes, it is. Just a moment, please."

Eurica retrieved a file from the shelves behind the counter before holding out a license that had Mira's name, class, and rank on it. "This should be it. If you could confirm all the information is spelled correctly, please?"

Mira peered at the laminated card.

Name: Mira

Class: Summoner

And thanks to the letter of recommendation, *Rank: C*

"Looks correct."

Opening a drawer, Eurica withdrew a rather simple-looking bracelet and placed it on the table. "Miss Mira, since you are Rank C, you also have the option to rent a User's Bangle. Would you like one?"

A User's Bangle... Mira seemed to remember hearing that term before. Seeing it before her, Mira recalled that Captain Astol had called her Control Terminals by that name when she'd run across his Magic-Clad Knights battling goblins on her first day back in this world.

"Hrmm, same as this?" Mira asked as she rolled up her left sleeve to show the bracelet clasped about her thin, pale wrist.

Eurica was stunned for a moment, but she regained her composure once more and nodded in agreement. After all, why shouldn't the pupil of Danblf have her own User's Bangle already?

"Indeed, that it is. I see you already have one."

"Hrmm."

User's Bangles were replicas of the original players' Control Terminals, but they lacked many of the functionalities. The reproductions were largely limited to Item Box access. Even so, the convenience they provided was immeasurable, and the guild would rent sets to adventurers of C-Rank and greater.

With secretive manufacturing techniques, their high production costs made them prohibitively expensive, and adventurers who owned a personal set were few and far between. That Mira possessed a set already was further proof in Eurica's mind that the girl was the genuine article.

Perking back up, Eurica opened the file and removed a sheet of paper, which she handed to Mira.

"Here's a summary of your rights and responsibilities as a member of the Mages' Guild, as well as our bylaws. Each quest is given a rank, and you cannot accept quests that are above your current rank. However, you may join in higher-ranked quests taken by those with an appropriate rank. If you do so, we ask that you sufficiently prepare for the tasks ahead."

She went on, "Furthermore, the various dungeons have rank-based restrictions. The entry wards are managed by the local guild office, so please inform the guild when you wish to enter. You will be issued a one-time permit that will allow you passage through the ward. Violation of the rules will cause you to be subject to penalties, so please take care."

Eurica paused her well-rehearsed disclaimer speech. "Do you have any questions about any of this so far?"

"I need to inform the guild, eh?" Mira stroked her chin and thought about the next step in her mission. "I'll be heading to the catacombs...er, the Ancient Temple Nebrapolis after this. How do I go about getting permission from the guild?"

"Wow! You're diving right in. Let's see..." Eurica craned her neck to look down the line of counters. "Dungeon Management is the counter to the far right of the entrance. You can apply for entry permission there."

"I see." Mira leaned to confirm the position of the counter in question. Her height and the crowded lobby made it difficult to see, but she spotted the desk past a cluster of people on the right-hand side.

"Finally," Eurica continued, "usage of basic guild facilities is free, and we offer discounts on food, drink, and other consumables. Damage will result in the repair cost being deducted from future compensation, so please treat our facilities with care."

Her spiel finished, Eurica pulled something from her pocket, about the same size as the license card. It was a cute pink card case made from leather and embossed with a ribbon and a wand.

"Um, this is a personal present. Please use it to carry your adventurer's license."

"S-sure. Thanks."

It was a bit girly for Mira's tastes, but Eurica's wide smile made it impossible to refuse. Mira just nodded politely in acceptance. Eurica quickly slipped the license into the case, sat it on the tray, and slid it across the counter to Mira.

Mira took the card case with a sour grin.

"Also, the guild leader said that he had something for you. It should be done by the end of the day, so he was hoping you would be able to drop by again tomorrow or whenever it's convenient for you."

"Something for me?"

"Indeed. He didn't tell me what it was, but he did say it came on behalf of King Solomon."

"Solomon, huh? All right, then. I'll drop by later."

"Thank you."

Mira had no idea what Leoneil wanted to give her, but it must have been related to her mission from Solomon.

"Well, that concludes our business today. For discretion's sake, only the guild leader and myself have been informed about your situation, Miss Mira. If there's anything further that I can help with, just let me know."

"Sure, sure."

"Also..."

"What now?" Mira felt like this was the conversation that would never end.

Whatever it was she wanted to say, Eurica was having a hard time saying it. But her eyes glittered with expectation as she looked at Mira. Finally, she blurted out, "Would you please shake my hand?!"

With a deep bow, she thrust her right hand out before her. Up until this point, she'd managed to maintain her professional demeanor, but now that the business was finally concluded, she couldn't contain it any longer.

Eurica was a fanatic when it came to the Nine Wise Men—Danblf in particular. Her house was packed with related merchandise and memorabilia. She'd even taken pilgrimages to Silverhorn and spent hours staring up at the Linked Silver Towers.

With the disciple of a legendary figure standing before her, she was completely beside herself.

"Uh, sure...?" Taken aback by the sudden display of fervor, Mira reached out and gently but firmly grasped her hand as tears welled up in Eurica's eyes.

"Ohmigod. I'll never wash my hand again!"

"Er, no, please do. Really," Mira said hesitantly, unsure whether to be flattered or frightened.

"Now, then, I hope you have a wonderful adventuring experience," said Eurica, snapping back into professionalism. "And thank you for your visit!"

After the energetic goodbye, Mira made her way to the rightmost counter. Many other mages stood between her and her destination, and she couldn't help but marvel at their outfits as she passed.

"I'm looking to get permission to enter the Ancient Temple. Can I do that here?" Mira said, still distractedly gawking at her fellow guildmates.

"Yes, I can help you with that," came a familiar voice.

Mira turned to stare across the counter—and there was Eurica. The desk's usual attendant stood in the background looking confused and annoyed, having been suddenly elbowed away from her post.

With her mouth still hanging open in surprise, Mira started to fill out the paperwork that Eurica slid across the counter.

A few minutes later, with the formalities completed and the fee of a thousand ducats paid, Eurica cheerfully issued Mira a permit to enter the Ancient Temple.

The permit itself seemed odd—simply a small card with the name of the dungeon and a sigil traced onto its surface in ink. Eurica explained that by touching the card to the ward stone at the entrance to the dungeon, the barrier would relax and allow access to the adventurer and their party. Ten seconds after the card was removed, the ward would be restored. And since the ward only prevented entry, no card was necessary to exit the dungeon.

Each card could only be used once. Adventurers needed to file an application every time they intended to reenter the dungeon and obtain a new entry permit.

That said, the cards could be recycled after undergoing a special process performed by the guild. Adventurers were asked to not throw them away, but rather to return them to the guild office upon their return.

"We're running low on cards at the moment, so it's very important to bring them back," Eurica concluded by pointing to a recycling box stationed near the entrance.

Mira nodded along to the explanation, and after a final handshake, she walked back outside onto the main street. She pulled her card case from her pouch and slid her precious dungeon pass within. The design might have been a bit girly, but it certainly was functional.

As she closed the case, the door to the Fighters' Guild burst open and the young boy from earlier came flying out again. His eyes were filled with tears, and he dashed off in Mira's direction without looking.

"Oof!" he gasped as he barreled straight into Mira's back, sending the case falling from her hand. Thankfully, she managed to stay on her feet.

"Whoa! What the heck was that about?!" Mira spun to confront whoever had bumped into her, only to see the young boy sniveling at her feet. Her anger cooled, and she bent down to put her arms around him and hoist him back to his feet.

"You okay, kid? Are you hurt?" she asked gently as she brushed him off.

The boy looked at Mira, his sorrow tinged with confusion. With a soft smile, Mira used the sleeve of her coat to wipe tears away from his red eyes. He seemed almost used to being spoiled.

"I'm fine. I'm sorry I ran into you." He sniffled, bowing his head.

Mira gave him a pat and responded, "That's all right."

"Are you injured, miss?" Mira looked up at the question to see a familiar elven woman with dark hair and dark eyes. "Ah, it's you. From yesterday."

The boy took a quick peek at the swordswoman but quickly dropped his gaze and trembled.

She clearly recognized the boy as well. "Based on the look on his face, I don't think he's crying because of the fall. Has he been trying to convince you too?"

If the tumble were the only issue, Mira would have just

offered the child an apple au lait and sent him on his way. But the boy's eyes were bright red, evidence that he'd been crying for some time. Mira was intrigued as to the reason.

"Oh, right, we haven't been properly introduced, have we?" said the elven woman. "I'm Emella."

"And I'm Mira." Mira stuck with her customary short introduction, then turned and wiped the boy's face again with the light admonishment. "Come now, boys shouldn't cry like this."

"Anyway, as for the reason..." Emella offered an embarrassed smile. "Well, it's not my fault. Not entirely. But there's really nothing I can do."

"Oh? And what might the reason be?" Mira asked with a hint of anger.

"I had to turn down his ridiculous request," Emella replied. "I mean, he's looking to enter a C-Rank dungeon. I'm a C-Rank adventurer, and I can get the permit, so he asked me. But seriously, I can't take a child into a dungeon!"

"Hrmm, I see." Mira's anger faded, seeing as Emella's reasoning made good sense.

Emella sighed in relief and flashed her adventurer's license as proof of her story. She was indeed a C-Rank adventurer and the license indicated that her class was swordsman. Mira had suspected as much, based on Emella's appearance.

"Checks out. Truth be told, I just joined the guild myself."

"Oh, so you're a newbie."

As Mira went to present her own freshly issued identification papers, she remembered what had just happened. Glancing around her feet, she muttered, "Oops, looks like I dropped my license."

"Oh, I'm sorry. That was my fault," the boy said, joining her in the hunt. He found the pink case first and as he scooped it from the street. As he did, it opened to reveal the dungeon permit.

"Miss! Miss, you're going to Nebrapolis?!" he asked, his face lighting up as he wiped at his eyes.

"Indeed, I am." Mira nodded, relieved for the simple reason that the boy had stopped crying.

"What...? No way!" Emella exclaimed. "You just joined, right? Shouldn't you only be G-Rank?"

The elven swordswoman jumped back in shock. It was unheard of for an adventurer to be C-Rank upon registration. Even with a recommendation, entry promotions topped out at E-Rank.

Advancement from G-Rank to E-Rank was largely a formality. Beyond that point, registered adventurers were only promoted based on their experience and abilities. To reach C-Rank meant that an adventurer had been recognized as top-notch and worthy of adventuring on an advanced level.

Somehow, this girl had vaulted straight to the upper tiers.

What in the world is going on?! was the only thought in Emella's mind as she raced over to stare at the card case the boy was still holding. But Mira's adventurer's license listed her as C-Rank, and there was no denying she also had a pass for the Ancient Temple Nebrapolis.

"But how...? A rookie can't... What?" sputtered Emella, flabbergasted. "A permit for the Ancient temple... And it's legit."

Even if someone tried to present false credentials, the information was still double-checked by the guild when applying for dungeon permits. The entry pass was impossible to forge—yet a C-Rank newbie with a dungeon pass was equally impossible. Emella muttered to herself, still confused, but the boy's eyes shone even brighter as he turned and bowed deeply to Mira.

"Miss, please, I'm begging you. Take me to Nebrapolis!" He was clearly desperate. If they hadn't been causing a scene before, now they certainly were. He bowed his head and uttered "please" over and over again.

"Hrmm, for what purpose?" Mira asked, intrigued as to why he was willing to risk the obvious dangers of the catacombs. Perhaps she could be the solution to his problem.

The boy looked up, his expression filled with anxiety and expectation—but also full of conviction.

"They say that in the deepest reaches of Nebrapolis, there's a mirror that lets you talk to the dead. That's where I need to go!"

"The Mirror of Darkness, eh?" Mira put a finger to her chin. "And who are you looking to find there?"

"I want to see my mother and father. My parents are both adventurers. But the Adventurers' Guild Union came and told me they've been missing for too long. They said my parents are officially dead." The boy fought back sniffles as he explained, and Mira gave him another quiet pat.

"Per guild rules, if an adventurer goes missing during a quest and isn't heard from for five years, they're considered killed in action," explained Emella. Judging by her expression, she was likely thinking of Thomas.

After being told he would never see them again, the boy would naturally want nothing else. So for the past week, he'd been showing up at the Fighters' Guild to ask adventurers for their help. Emella had seen him there several times and thus became aware of what was going on.

"I see, so that's the situation." Mira gently placed her hand on the boy's head. She spoke softly and looked him in the eyes with a reassuring smile. "Lucky for you, I was heading there anyway. Might as well bring you along."

He stared at her in disbelief before blinking back fresh tears and breaking into a wide smile.

"Th-thank you so very much! By the way, my name is Tact!"

5

HAVING GRANTED HIS TRUEST WISH, Mira grasped Tact's hand and began to briskly walk away. Emella stared after them in horror before shouting at the pair.

"Whoa, hold up a minute! Are you planning on going with just the two of you?!" she yelled as she sprinted around to block their path.

"That's the idea," came Mira's immediate reply, stunning Emella again for a moment before she could regain her bearings.

"You can't take a child with no combat experience into a C-Rank dungeon!"

Emella's reasoning was sound. Gods knew it was reckless to take a child into *any* dungeon, and the difference in danger between a D-Rank and a C-Rank dungeon was massive. Everyone in the guild would agree—as evidenced by Tact's continuous rejections.

"He'll be fine as long as I'm protecting him." Mira's words were blunt, and she had no interest in (or experience with) the guild's policies. Even with an escort in tow, she knew that her skills alone were more than enough to handle whatever arose on their journey to the fifth level of the catacombs.

"How can you be so rash?" Emella agonized over Mira's confidence. Somehow, this magical girl was showing more bravado than even battle-worn veterans.

A spellcaster's abilities weren't measured by their appearance—she knew that much. But even assuming that Mira was a skilled mage, Emella couldn't comprehend why the girl was taking the situation so lightly. Was it false bravado...or could she truly back it up? Emella had no way of knowing.

Mira was a C-Rank, despite being a rookie adventurer who had just registered with the guild. That was so unprecedented that it was clear she had to have some amazing skill. But Emella also couldn't dismiss her trepidation that Mira was simply being reckless. Finally, she made up her mind.

"Very well, then I'm going with you!"

Mira nodded in agreement, deciding that this compromise was better than standing in the street and arguing about it all morning.

With Emella's decision made, the three retreated to a café to hash out the details. The establishment was called Café du Chocolat, and its menu was true to its name.

"So I have to ask, what type of mage are you? I mean, you are a mage, right, Mira?"

Emella's first point of order was trying to discern Mira's abilities. Since the Ancient Temple Nebrapolis was filled with undead, certain types of magic users would have an advantage there. Were

Mira a priestess or an exorcist, she would have the upper hand against the monsters...and that would go a long way toward explaining her boundless self-confidence.

"I'm a summoner," Mira said before turning back to the café's signature dish, the Chocolatique Overload.

Emella had ordered it for Mira as a treat, but it was a bit large. The little summoner was currently sharing it with Tact, and occasionally, she would reach over with a napkin to wipe whipped cream off his face. Despite the cute sibling vibe, Emella's expression was frozen in place.

Summoners as a class were practically extinct. Emella didn't know of anyone who was pursuing the discipline, other than a few scholars employed by the Linked Silver Towers.

After staring at Mira for a few moments, perplexed, she managed to ask, "Um, I'm not the most well versed, but are summoners...strong?"

Mira felt her pride swell at the question, but she also remembered her conversation with Cleos, acting Elder of the Tower of Evocation. The summoning arts had faded away. Emella was a C-Rank adventurer—clearly considered someone of great skill!—yet she spoke as if she'd never seen a summoner in combat.

Looking up to the heavens, Mira pursed her lips. To think the world had come to this! She resolved to reclaim the dignity and respect of her discipline with her own two hands.

"You'll understand when the time is right," she replied with a faint smile.

The response only served to increase Emella's anxiety. "I'd rather understand before it's too late," she grumbled.

Their chat concluded, the three left Café du Chocolat.

"Well, then, let's get going, shall we?" Mira proposed, squinting in the bright sunlight. Taking Tact by the hand, she set off in the direction of the Ancient Temple, leaving Emella standing behind them, her face frozen in shock.

What have I gotten myself into? she asked herself silently as despair threatened to overwhelm her.

"Hold up! You do understand we're talking about a C-Rank dungeon, right? We can't just go strolling in there unprepared. It will take us at least a day to get things ready."

That should have been common sense. Everyone knew it took time to prepare, and for advanced dungeoneering, it sometimes took up to a week. What was Mira thinking if she planned to head off the same day?

Mira paused to consider it. "Very well, then. We'll set off tomorrow." She had planned to complete the expedition within the day but was willing to make the concession—it was a minor annoyance, but the hotel was comfortable enough, and she wouldn't mind having another night's rest.

That meant it was time for Emella, experienced adventurer extraordinaire, to show her stuff.

She insisted that the party should go shopping for supplies, and she knew all the stores to visit. From necessary restoratives to adventuring equipment, her knowledge was encyclopedic. If the need arose, she was more than prepared to use every last potion and tool to cover their escape. She dutifully showed Tact the basics of how to use each purchase, so he could assist as a last resort.

Conversely, Mira bought some bug repellent.

"Are you sure that's enough, Mira?" Emella asked.

"Of course. I've been planning this trip for a while. Everything I need is in here." Mira rolled up her left sleeve to display her Control Terminal, or the User's Bangle, as it was known to the natives of this world.

Her statement was technically true, but not reassuring in the slightest.

"That's all well and good but..." Emella added a few extra potions to her purchase, just in case.

With the shopping taken care of, the trio made their way to the food market. Emella made a beeline for one shop in particular.

"Well, if it isn't Emella. Come on in," called a sturdily built woman from the back of the stall. Its shelves were lined with prepared foods and seasonings. "Where are you off to this time?"

Emella couldn't help but smile back at the friendly greeting. "We're heading to the Ancient Temple tomorrow."

"Oho! Big trip, eh? With your guild, you'll be fine, but do take care, all right? I'd hate to lose my favorite customer!"

"Of course! Thank you." Emella pointedly didn't mention that Mira and Tact would be joining the expedition, but the shopkeeper still turned an appraising eye on the pair.

"I didn't know you had kids," the grocer said with a twinkle in her eye.

"I absolutely don't!" Emella blushed and sputtered at the jest.

As Emella spoke with the shopkeeper, she placed a selection of dried meats, freeze-dried vegetables, and canned fruits on the counter. Mira kept an ear to the banter of the two while perusing the wares to see if anything looked particularly tasty.

The next stop was the armory. Weapons and armor crafted from various metals lined the walls. Customers browsed the selection, stopping occasionally to check the condition of the goods.

"So, Mira, you aren't carrying any obvious weapons," Emella said, knowing that if Mira did use any sort of weapon, it would be stashed inside her User's Bangle. "What kind of weapons do summoners usually wield?"

Most adventurers kept their weapons within easy reach in case of emergency. Emella unconsciously placed her hand on the pommel of the sword strapped to her hip.

"Don't need one. Summoning is my weapon."

"Oh. Really, now?"

That might have been true for Mira, but many summoners carried staves or wands to increase their store of mana and recovery rate. Mira's abilities had surpassed those needs years ago, and more importantly, she was dual-classed as a Sage. Sages fought barehanded, and holding a staff would prevent her from using her full range of attacks.

But Emella knew even less of Sages than she did of summoners, so she chalked it up to another of Mira's idiosyncrasies as she browsed the armory for armor in Tact's size. So far, she had been covering most of the purchases out of her own pocket. It didn't seem right to let children fend for themselves.

Mira did nothing to correct that notion.

Shopping finally complete, Emella plopped herself down on the stone fence surrounding the monument to the deceased that stood in the town square. The sun had dipped beneath the horizon, and streetlamps illuminated the shapes of townsfolk on their way home beneath an indigo sky.

"Well, that should do it...even if I would have preferred more time to prepare," she said with a tired sigh. "We planned for tomorrow, but shall we meet in front of the guild buildings at ten?"

"Indeed," muttered Mira as she hopped up on the low stone fence herself.

Tact bowed deeply to the two women. "Yes! I'll be there!"

Emella's smile concealed the worry she had about tomorrow's expedition. Even with the preparations, she wasn't entirely comfortable with the situation.

"Well, it is getting quite late, so why don't we call it a day?" she suggested. "Where do the two of you live?"

"I live with my grandpa. His house is behind the guild buildings."

"And I...hrmm, where was it again?" Mira realized she hadn't bothered to learn the name of the hotel she was staying at. Even if she asked an officer for directions, she wouldn't know what to say. "'The best hotel in town,' I think he said."

She absentmindedly stroked her chin while trying to remember what Garrett had told her.

Emella had to steady herself on the fence to keep from falling off and put a hand to her forehead in exasperation. Tact just tilted his head to the side, puzzled.

Sighing, Emella pointed up at a massive building across the town square, which was lit up by streetlights. The sight of the hotel at night was an entirely different wonder compared to the daylight spectacle.

"Ah, yes, that's the place. I didn't realize it was so close." Mira nodded as she spotted the familiar yet altogether different façade of the hotel.

"I just...don't even know why I'm surprised," Emella mumbled as she stood and took Tact by the hand. "Well then, I'll see you home, Tact. You should head back too, all right, Mira?"

As Emella spoke, she stared Mira straight in the eyes until Mira looked away in discomfort.

"I-indeed. I am quite hungry after all, so I think I'll be on my way," Mira said, backing away from Emella, who was suddenly a little too close for comfort. Despite her current form, she couldn't help but get a little flustered being so close to a stunningly beautiful woman.

"That sounds like a wonderful idea. We'll see you tomorrow."

"Right, tomorrow it is. I'll see you tomorrow as well, Tact. Get a good night's sleep."

"Thank you so much, Miss Mira! I'll see you tomorrow."

"Hrmm."

Completing her farewell with a curt nod, Mira turned and walked off toward the hotel. Emella watched until Mira had entered the building's front gate before she tugged on Tact's hand and led him in the direction of the guild buildings.

She Professed Herself Herself Pupil of the Wise Man

6

THE WINDOWS HAD BEEN thrown open to allow a warm breeze to flow through the lobby as Mira descended the next morning. The weather was picnic-worthy, and she was in high spirits as she anticipated the upcoming adventure—finally, a chance to show off the true essence and power of the summoning arts!

After retrieving a packed lunch from the dining hall, Mira walked out of the hotel and into the crowded town square where villagers and adventurers were going about their business. Making her way to the meeting place in front of the guild, Mira looked around for Emella and Tact. It seemed that both had yet to arrive, so she made herself comfortable on one of the chairs outside the Mages' Guild.

"Hrmm, what's all that?" she muttered a moment later as she saw a boisterous throng of onlookers.

Men and women, young and old, were clustered around something in the small square before the guild buildings. She wondered if it was another zombie, but the sudden cries and cheers emanating from the crowd quickly put that theory to rest.

Losing her interest, Mira pulled out an apple au lait and sipped at it absentmindedly. Soon, the large clock in the plaza showed ten o'clock—their planned meeting time—and yet her companions were nowhere to be seen.

"What's the holdup? Why are they both late?"

Mira searched the square to make sure they weren't posted up at a different location, and she noticed the strange gathering was still milling about.

Some sort of street performance? she wondered as she stood to investigate. Just as she did, a rather familiar young boy came bursting out of the crowd, tripping over an errant foot and dropping the two copper coins in his hand. He immediately scrambled after them.

"Well, if it isn't Tact. What are you up to?" she asked, stooping to snatch one of the rolling coins.

"Oh, Miss Mira. Good morning!" he replied as Mira held out the wayward coin. His smile was radiant.

"That accounts for you, but where's Emella?"

"Oh, she's over there." Tact pointed back at the crowd.

That made sense; Emella must have arrived earlier and was killing time by watching whatever performance was going on in the crowd's center.

"Miss Emella! I found Miss Mira!" Tact yelled out as he ran back into the mob.

A few moments later, Emella shouldered her way out of the crowd as well.

"Oh, you're here. You should have said something."

"Are you serious? How was I to know you were caught up in all that?" Mira shrugged and sighed.

Emella turned and looked back, smiling wryly as she clasped her hands together in apology. "I'm sorry! I never imagined so many people would show up!"

Something seemed suspicious about the proffered excuse, but just as Mira opened her mouth to comment on it, another voice interjected.

"So is this the girl the vice captain was going on about?" The crowd parted, allowing a large man to pass through.

He stood and looked over Emella's shoulder at Mira. His heavy metal armor shone with a dull luster and he wore a gauntlet decorated with a scarlet bell. A metal war hammer slung across his back was nearly as long as the man was tall, and it spoke to his uncommon physical strength—yet he had a good-natured look about him. His close-cropped red hair and stubble lent him a wild, rough-cut edge.

"Ohmigod, she's adorable!" squealed a woman in purple robes, bouncing up and down to Emella's right.

Behind blue-rimmed glasses, her green eyes shone with desire. A scarlet bell was embroidered on her sleeve, and Mira realized this must be the emblem of their guild. Hanging at her waist was a staff nearly a meter long.

A quick glance at her face, framed by green hair that hung just below her shoulders, would give the impression of some intelligence...but her disturbingly lecherous grin ruined the effect.

"Seriously?! Where?!" called another man as he pushed his way forward through the throng. "Whoa, cutie alert! A little on the young side for my taste, but maybe in a few years..."

Mira returned the lightly armored man's up-down look with one of mild disgust. He had ear piercings and brown hair tucked under a green bandana, which was decorated with the now-familiar scarlet bell. Despite his lack of manners and flirtatious flair, he was tall and handsome. Two daggers sat on his hip, and he wore an open-front black jacket and camouflage pants held up by several belts.

"Who's this?" Mira asked in annoyance with the sweep of a hand to indicate the three newcomers. The only thing she knew was that they were obviously acquaintances of Emella.

"These are my guildmates! The Écarlate Carillon's finest!" Emella responded, clearly proud of her friends and companions.

"More like the only ones available to take the job," the handsome rogue muttered with a sly grin.

"What was that?!" Emella turned to lightly punch him as he immediately began trying to play it off as a joke.

"I'm Asval. Well met, young lady," the large man said, undeterred. His stern face was belied by a faint smile and a voice filled with warmth.

"And I'm Flicker! Nice to meet you." The young woman adjusted her glasses with one hand and offered her other.

"I-indeed. I'm Mira." Mira reached forward warily to shake Flicker's hand.

The moment they touched, Flicker broke back into her lecherous grin. With unexpected strength, she tugged Mira in for a firm embrace. Mira found herself trapped in Flicker's arms.

"Little adorable Mira, is it?" Flicker gushed. "Look at how pudgy your cheeks are! Ohmigod, you're *so* adorable."

Mira moved to escape, but she was held in Flicker's vise grip as the other magician poked and prodded at her cheeks. Her evasions were useless, and the pokes kept coming.

"Emella, do something!" was all Mira managed to say as she squirmed in Flicker's hold.

Emella turned from scolding the playboy and smiled bitterly before smacking Flicker over the head with a forceful chop.

"Sorry about that, Mira. I asked her to keep her hands to herself."

"Yes, I'd prefer as little of that as possible," said Mira as she took the opportunity to jump away from Flicker.

The blow must have been quite powerful—Flicker was holding her head with both hands and looked to be in agony. Despite that, she was still trying to move closer to Mira, but Asval stepped in to put himself between them.

"I'm Zephard. But you can call me Zef!" said the rogue with a dashing smile. He'd managed to sneak up behind Mira noiselessly, and she turned to find him kneeling down to match her height. Mira was startled but impressed.

"I'm Mira," she blurted out as usual before turning to Emella once more. "So why are they here?"

Guildmates hadn't been part of yesterday's planning session.

"They're here to help!" Emella responded, as though it were obvious.

To Mira, the Ancient Temple might not be anything more than a low-level hunting ground, but for everyone else, it was a real threat. No one in their right mind would venture into a C-Rank dungeon without a full party. After they parted ways the previous evening, Emella had rushed to recruit her guildmates for the adventure.

Mira wasn't opposed to the additions—quite the contrary, in fact. It had been a long time since she'd PUGed with randoms. Their surprise appearance caused her a pleasant twinge of nostalgia.

"Hrmm, very well. Shall we set forth?" Grabbing Tact's hand, she began to walk off, only to find her path blocked by a wall of onlookers on every side.

Écarlate Carillon was a guild of renown, and when four key members of the group appeared together, they were bound to attract attention. Now that the group had an adorable girl in tow, the crowd's interest level grew even more.

"Miss Emella, you're amazing!"

"Give us a pun, Flicker!"

"Don't get too cocky, Zef!"

"Next round is on you, brother Asval!"

"Is that girlie a new member?"

"Hey, Zef, be careful walking home at night!"

Cheers and jeers came from all sides, but the guildmates were clearly used to it. Emella waved at the crowd while Asval smiled and laughed. For her part, Flicker stayed focused on Mira. Zef tried to keep a low profile—an impossible task given the circumstances.

"Always the same old abuse," he muttered.

"All right, you lot! Follow me!" called Emella above the noise of the crowd. With her right hand raised, she advanced forward and the crowd parted to clear a path. The party departed to shouts of encouragement.

"Yes, ma'am!"

Mira lurked in the safety of Asval's shadow and marveled at the level of celebrity these adventurers seemed to have.

An hour later, the sounds of Karanak had fallen behind them and they passed through a forest to the north of the city. As they emerged into a clearing at the base of a cliff, a series of giant statues stood to meet them. Countless forms had been carved directly into the rock wall, which stretched out in a line far beyond where their eyes could see. They looked human at first glance, but closer inspection revealed this was not the case.

Before them lay the entrance to the Ancient Temple Nebrapolis.

"Well, time to get to it," said Emella as she looked up at the statues and steeled herself for what was to come. "Zef, you're up first."

Mira's demeanor was quite the opposite. She gawked at the scenery like a tourist, squaring her memories against the reality laid out before her.

"Okay, off I go," said the rogue as he muffled his footsteps and slipped into the temple.

Though unlikely, there was always a chance that monsters might lurk inside the ritual hall serving as the dungeon's gateway. The party waited patiently outside until Zephard's voice echoed, "All clear!"

The rest of the party entered the ritual chamber and found a spot to relax after their march from Karanak. After a short breather, Emella addressed the group.

"Okay, let's go over the plan once more. Our target is the Hall of Darkness on the fifth level. That's where we'll find the Mirror of Darkness."

"With all due respect, Miss Mira," said Asval, "I'm not all too familiar with summoning techniques, and the fifth level is home to some heavy hitters. Will we be able to handle that?"

Écarlate Carillon had delved into this dungeon before, and every member knew it took a well-equipped and well-prepared party of experienced adventurers to make it to the bottom. They were some of the guild's best, but there were only four of them and a summoner of unknown ability. Asval's frank question wasn't unfounded.

"Hrmm. Looks like I'm going to make this raid an educational experience," Mira boasted with a smug smile.

If Écarlate Carillon had the celebrity and status that she suspected, then convincing its members to recognize the power of the summoning arts it would be another step toward restoring her discipline to its former glory.

"Really, now? I look forward to it!" Asval said as he rechecked the party's potions and various tools.

"Asval and I will take the vanguard. Mira, Tact, you stay in the middle. Flicker and Zef will follow up in the rear, all right?" Emella looked at each member in turn to confirm that they understood the plan.

"Understood," said Asval, inspecting the grip of his war hammer.

"Got it!" chirped Flicker as she shuffled through a deck of what looked like tarot cards.

"Aye aye," came Zephard's response. He was smearing some sort of oil on his daggers.

"Okay! Yes, ma'am!" Tact looked both hopeful and apprehensive at the same time.

For her part, Mira simply gave an aloof wave of her hand and muttered, "Fine by me."

Emella nodded with satisfaction at each answer before removing the sword and scabbard from her waist and placing it into her Item Box. Then she withdrew a different weapon and hooked it to her arming belt with a satisfied smile.

"Hey, isn't that the captain's blade?" asked Asval as he saw it. The rest of the group looked up in surprise.

"Indeed, it is," Emella said, pulling the sword from the scabbard. The double edges shone with a pale white light and tiny motes of stardust fell from the weapon's edge, dimming as they made their way toward the stone floor. "When I told him where we were headed, he let me borrow it. This should greatly improve our chances in here."

"Oho. Is that a light spirit blade? Very nice, indeed." Mira stepped closer to look at the sword.

"Well spotted! It belongs to the captain, but like I said, he lent it to me." Emella looked mesmerized by the sword. As she returned it to its scabbard, the flecks of light clinging to the blade were extinguished.

The pale white shine was a giveaway that the blade was light-attuned—but this blade bore a rather unique history. While most light-attuned swords were created by adding pyroxene ore to the alloy, Mira could tell that this was a much rarer holy sword of exceptional quality. While a warrior like Emella could tell the blade was special, a mage such as Mira would be able to determine more specific qualities of the weapon.

Each spirit blade bore the holy blessing of the individual spirit that sanctified it, and the weapon would bear specific modifiers related to the spirit involved. Armor could be blessed as well, though that was less common.

While Emella, Asval, and Zef might have thought Mira well-read, Flicker cocked her head and looked at the girl with an appraising eye. Only a powerful mage could have made that discernment at a glance.

"I'll leave the heavy lifting to you, then!" Asval smirked as he stood, hammer slung across his back once more.

"Don't threaten me with a good time!" Emella grinned back before calling to the rest of the party, "Let's go!"

Following her boisterous call, the rest of the party surged to their feet, and they headed toward the altar, which served as the entrance to the first level. The altar supported a conspicuous-looking crystal ball, and the air beyond seemed to be covered by an opaque film, looking almost like frosted glass.

Taking a step forward, Mira pulled her card case from her pouch and thought back to Eurica's instructions. She pressed the entry permit to the surface of the crystal, and instantly, the film vanished to reveal a set of stone steps descending into the dungeon.

"Hrmm, neat trick," Mira muttered as she stared at the permit. The sigil had vanished, leaving only the name of the dungeon embossed on the card. Mira returned the blank card to her case.

One by one, the party descended the stairs, with Mira bringing up the rear.

"All right, here we go! Wonder if we'll find any loot?" called Zephard.

"Don't get ahead of yourself," admonished Asval. "We're here to escort them to the Hall of Darkness."

"Yeah, I know."

She
Professed
Herself
Pupil of the
Wise Man

MIRA AND THE REST OF THE PARTY found themselves walking down a long, gloomy corridor lit by the flickering, pallid light of lanterns hanging from the guildmember's belts. Each lantern consisted of a metal cage enclosed around a floating sphere, which gave off a pale blue glow.

"Well, those certainly lit the place," Mira muttered to no one in particular.

"I didn't bother going to the adventurers' supply shop because you said your equipment was taken care of," Emella griped. "I never thought you'd come here without a lantern."

Mira smirked, and a moment later, a brilliant ball of light appeared above her head. "Every mage should be able to cast a common light spell. It's a fundamental technique."

"That may be...but are you sure you should be wasting your mana without knowing what's ahead?" Emella heaved a sigh of exasperation.

Flicker nodded in agreement. Squandering precious mana

when a standard lantern would suffice was unthinkable for an adventuring mage.

"The mana requirement for this spell is trivial," Mira replied.

"Is that so?" The ways of the summoner were inscrutable to Emella, so she figured it must be some class benefit.

As for Flicker, if Mira could see spirit traces which she herself could not, then she wasn't in a position to object.

The spell didn't last forever and had to be recast when it went out. While she was satisfied to show off at the moment, Mira was nostalgic for Danblf's adventures with Cleos back in the good old days. As a light spirit, Cleos illuminated even the darkest regions of a dungeon like the noonday sun. As she walked down the corridor, she wondered if having him here now would make their journey easier, or if it would simply unsettle her companions.

In any case, the spell wasn't a class benefit, but Mira's pool of mana had already bounced back from the cost. As one of the Wise Men, her maximum value and recovery rate far outstripped that of the common adventurers.

The conversation hushed as the party reached the end of the corridor, where it opened into a small room.

The air against their skin was damp, and the far side of the room was shrouded in silent darkness. Pulling out her map, Emella checked the directions to the next waypoint, and they continued on. Nothing but the repetitive sounds of breathing, footsteps, and plates of armor rubbing together followed along with them.

Almost time for the monsters to start appearing, thought Mira as she ran her fingers along the stone wall. *Down one more set of stairs, through the first hall, then down the next corridor into the atrium. Then we'll have a fight on our hands.*

[Evocation: Holy Knight]

Setting the summoning point next to herself, she prepared for battle. A glowing magic circle appeared on the floor, illuminating the corridor.

"What's that light?!" cried a startled Emella.

"What is it? What's wrong?!" shouted Asval as he wheeled and brandished his war hammer to engage whatever foe had ambushed the party. As he did, he saw a pure white knight step out of a circle of light.

"Sorry about that. Just needed to summon a spirit." Mira rapped her knuckles against the armored faulds at the knight's waist.

Her summoned spirit towered over her, nearly two meters tall, and carried both a giant white tower shield as well as a long silver sword. It was covered from head to toe in glimmering white armor; a flickering red light shone through the slit in the visor.

"Is that an armor spirit?" Emella asked in awe.

"You can feel its power." Flicker let out a gasp, reaching up to stroke the spirit's pauldron. The white knight was both overwhelmingly intimidating and somehow reassuring.

Zef couldn't help but blurt "That's so cool!" as he examined it from every angle.

"So this is summoning? You weren't kidding about this trip

being educational..." mused Asval, considering Emella's conversation with him the night before.

He recalled her story of how Mira had only just registered with the guild and yet had somehow been granted a C-Rank license. He figured that Emella must have been confused or mistaken...but then she told him that they were going to the Ancient Temple Nebrapolis.

With a creeping sense of dread, he wondered if the spirit standing before him was a sign of things to come.

Grinning, Mira ordered the Holy Knight to protect Tact and repel anyone or anything that approached the child with harmful intent. While the Dark Knight would have been her summoning of choice for solo adventuring, the Holy Knight was a spirit devoted to the art of defense. It could even outperform higher-level summons when used properly. With her Holy Knight active and vigilant against danger, Mira was confident that she could have escorted Tact to the lowest level of the dungeon without any help at all.

After that, the party made their way into the great hall. Asval led the way, checking the grip on his hammer and casting a wary glance at their surroundings. He froze and held up his hand to signal those following.

"Hold. I sense something up ahead."

Emella consulted her map while Zef moved up to provide close protection for Mira and Tact, taking a dagger in each hand.

Like ripples spreading across the still surface of a pond, the sound of dragging footsteps began to reverberate throughout the hall. Slowly but surely, they rose in intensity and frequency.

Weapons at the ready, Asval and Emella faced the darkness and guarded each other's flank. Zef kept a sharp eye on the rear to hedge against a possible ambush. Moving closer to Mira and Tact, Flicker calmed her mind and prepared to cast at the first sign of danger.

"Looks like we've got ghouls," said Asval, making no attempt to hide his disgust as the first silhouettes drew into their circle of light.

The two fighters suppressed their revulsion and squared off against the shambling monsters as the Holy Knight moved to place itself between the abominations and Tact. Shield in hand, the spirit would fight to the bitter end against the ghouls if it came to that.

But I don't favor their chances, Mira thought, letting a small smile spread on her lips.

Mira had become so accustomed to adventuring with Cleos that it had been a long while since she'd last experienced monsters emerging from the darkness. She strained to see the action, but Asval was blocking the end of the corridor, and no matter how she swayed from side to side, she was just a bit too short to get a good sight. Visuals aside, another of her senses was threatening to overwhelm the moment...

"Ugh! What a stench..."

Mira frowned at the foul odor that was growing in intensity.

It seemed that Tact smelled the same thing as he pinched his nose and whined, "Eww, what *is* that?"

"Just part of the full ghoul experience," Zef said cheerfully.

As the warriors held the creatures at bay, he explained that the putrid scent of rot was a ghoul's calling card. A parasitic entity, the monster latched onto corpses and reanimated them—but it couldn't restore life functions. The corpse continued to rot as the parasite controlled the body...at least until it fell to pieces and the ghoul was forced to find another dead host.

Mira's expression grew even more disgusted. She recoiled in shock as she managed to catch a glimpse of a ghoul around Asval's blocking form—a lump of flesh so festered and decayed that it was hard to even call it a corpse. Cloudy, unfocused eyes stared blankly ahead at its prey, and the gaping, lipless mouth revealed a tongue that looked almost ready to fall out. Only a few strands of hair remained attached to its peeling scalp. Torn skin revealed clumps of maggots writhing in the decayed flesh.

It was so gruesome, so barely human that even the air she breathed began to feel thick with corruption. Mira fought a horrible urge to vomit. But as she looked away, she caught a glimpse of Tact, and her pride gave her cause to swallow her nausea.

"I'll start us off," Flicker declared, and she stepped forward and cast the spell she'd been preparing.

[Sorcery: Truest Crimson]

Power gathered at the tip of her raised staff for an instant before a whirlpool of flame erupted between the two shambling forms. The ghouls' skin burned as their limbs withered in the conflagration, sending them falling to the ground. The flames followed them down, scattering their ashes and cremating the corpses thoroughly. It took but a few moments to immolate the pitiful husks and cleanse them of their impurity—even the stench was burned away.

Two more ghouls marched forward into the light as the flames subsided, and Asval and Emella leapt forward. Emella's sword slashed one of the unfortunate monsters in half while Asval's war hammer scattered pieces of rotten flesh and maggots to the corners of the room with a mighty blow.

"I think we're clear," he said a moment later when no other creeping horror emerged from the darkness. Tact peeked out from behind the shield of the Holy Knight, nose still firmly pinched shut.

The whole encounter lasted only a half-minute, but it served to reaffirm to Mira that this all was no longer a game—rather a reality that had dire consequences for anyone who faced it unprepared. Due to the visual realism of the game, she'd been unable to look directly at a ghoul the first time she encountered one. The effect had worn off over time—but the addition of the olfactory sense was something she was sure she'd never grow accustomed to.

The ghouls that'd been reduced to ash weren't an issue, but the two destroyed by Emella and Asval still reeked of decay. Mira's expression soured as she led Tact and her Holy Knight into the room to rejoin the warriors.

"Didn't you take your medicine, Tact?" asked Emella.

"I took it," he replied with a dutiful look on his face.

"Then the smell shouldn't be bothering you that much." She fixed the child with a skeptical gaze.

"Give him a break," Zephard interjected, then began poking around the ghouls' remains. "We may be used to it, but this is the kid's first time. Even with the medicine reducing the smell, some always lingers."

"That's true," Emella muttered as she thought back to her early days.

"Um...medicine?" Mira asked as she pulled the collar of her shirt over her mouth and nose to avoid the full brunt of the smell.

"The scent blockers. Wait, did you not bring any?!"

"Never heard of them."

"First the lanterns, now this..." Emella shook her head. "It's a drug that makes smelly things...*less smelly*."

"Simply put, but yeah, basically." Asval shrugged in agreement as he tossed aside a rag he'd used to clean the gore from his war hammer. "The medicine partially paralyzes the nerves in the nose—it doesn't block all smell, just sort of sets an upper limit on how bad things can get. It's been around for about twenty years now... I can't imagine what it was like killing these things before that."

Amazing. I wonder what else I'll discover? Curiosity fought with revulsion within Mira's thoughts.

The stench won.

Her focus returned to the present, surrounded by the odor of decay. Tact dared to remove his fingers, and it seemed that with the aid of the drug, he was able to somehow endure it.

A thought occurred to Mira—they were currently in the Ancient Temple Nebrapolis. The catacombs were an undead paradise, and the ghouls were just the opening volley. Things would only keep ramping up, and on the third level was the Giant Ghoul—a massive, rotting corpse. The smell would be indescribable.

The pretense of adventure and camaraderie was all well and good, but it was time to take matters into her own hands. She reached her right hand out to the side and pointed slightly away from the rest of the group.

[Summoning Arts: Bound Arcana]

As Mira spoke her spell, a blue magic circle as tall as herself appeared at her right hand—but Mira's spell wasn't done yet. Confirming the magic circle, she extended her other hand as well.

A second magic circle appeared, slowly turning and radiating power. Bound Arcana was a skill unique to summoners and served to supercharge summons that were near the magic circle. But Mira wasn't using this to enhance her one of her usual summoned spirits. Bound Arcana also served as a requirement for the technique she had in mind.

"Mira, what are you doing?" asked Emella, backing away slowly at the sight of the young girl wielding so much magic power.

"Just wait and see."

Mira began to draw her hands together and the circles followed.

[Summoning Arts: Mark of the Rosary]

As she touched the magic circles, they began to glow with blinding intensity, and a moment later, they were instantly rewritten. The rest of the party gasped in wonder.

The light receded, revealing a double magic circle larger than the previous two. Each circle glowed red, and powerful magic could be seen radiating from their centers. The rest of the party murmured in amazement, but Flicker stared at the sight in entranced silence and listened.

All high-level spells required chants to accompany the casting, and this one was no different. Mira touched one of the circles and slowly began to whisper:

I call upon the maiden of heaven.

She who wields the holy blade.

She who is called Alfina.

Who swore loyalty to her master.

Answer my call.

Though the words were nearly inaudible, a voice echoed through the room. The guildmates looked about before realizing that it came from where Mira stood.

[Evocation: Valkyrie]

The magic circles glowed in response to her power.

"What is this? What's going on?!" Emella cried, holding a hand up to shield her eyes.

But Flicker gazed directly into the brilliant scene, squinting to try to discern what sort of magic she was witnessing. The rest turned their faces away to avoid it and fought the urge to run.

The magic circles around Mira flared, then vanished. A moment later, another magic circle slowly appeared. It split into an upper and lower circle that separated to leave a pillar of light in between.

"I am here as you command. It has been some time, my master."

A solitary woman stepped out from the pillar of light. She was beautiful—clad in azure light armor, gauntlets, and greaves. Her ice-blue hair cascaded down her back in waves and was held back by a circlet around her forehead. The sword at her hip was carried in a scabbard of azure leather that matched her armor, but a divine light spilled from within.

The battle maiden stood expectantly before the party.

"Been a while, Alfina," Mira said, staring at the woman.

The summoned Valkyrie dropped to a knee before Mira to pay her respects.

"You've certainly changed, haven't you, Master?" Alfina cocked an eyebrow as she looked at Mira.

"Yeah, well...things happened." Mira expected some sort of reaction, but she still fought to hide any bitterness in her voice.

"Did they, now?"

Back in the game, spirits summoned via rituals only gave minimal responses to commands. But Alfina was engaging in conversation of her own volition, confirming another of Mira's suspicions—she wasn't dealing with mere NPCs anymore.

It wasn't an entirely unwelcome development for Mira, who had become accustomed to adventuring solo. It would be nice to have someone to talk to now and then—even if it was a person she'd summoned from thin air. Mira's face lit up as she realized that she'd no longer be lonely when soloing.

"How have you been, Alfina?" Mira asked, curious to how far the conversation might go.

"My sisters and I have been training daily so that we are prepared for whenever you call upon us."

"Hrmm, indeed. I see. Very commendable."

"I am honored by your praise, Master."

"Say, uh...Mira? Who is this?" With wide eyes pinned on the intimidating aura of the Valkyrie, Emella worked up the nerve to step forward and get some answers.

Flicker and Zef each stared for their own reasons—the former out of magical appreciation, the latter out of lust.

"Emella, meet Alfina." As Mira made introductions, Alfina stood and turned to face Emella with a slight bow. "Alfina, this is Emella."

"You must be one of my master's comrades. A pleasure."

Emella stammered, "L-likewise." She sketched a bow of her own in return.

"Well she's certainly a looker. And unlike the knight, she can talk." Asval had regained his bearings and muttered approvingly as he gazed at Alfina. Just as a mage could sense another mage's magical flow, the imposing warrior was astounded by the Valkyrie's incomparable battle aura.

"I told you this would be educational. I hope this has changed your opinion of summoners!" Crossing her arms, Mira puffed out her chest. She was convinced that she was well on her way to restoring the power of the summoning arts.

"Master, your orders?" Alfina asked, fearing that unless she took the initiative, she might become the subject of a lecture rather than a participant in battle.

"Go forth and cleanse all monsters between here and the fifth floor!" Mira replied, undoing all Emella's planning and preparation with a single order. She'd smelled enough ghoul for one day.

"As you command."

Drawing her sword from its scabbard, Alfina sprinted into the depths of the Ancient Temple while leaving a trail of azure light in her wake.

8

A FTER ALFINA HAD DEPARTED like a gale blowing across
the open sea, Mira blinked heavily to shake the image of the
ghouls from her mind. That problem should be solved.

"Shall we continue?" she asked, looking farther down the corridor at the fading azure light.

Tact rushed up to her side and took her hand. As if invited,
Flicker followed suit and took her other hand. Mira furrowed
her brow in dismay. Meanwhile, Emella, Asval, and Zef stood
frozen as they stared down the passageway where Alfina had
departed.

"Did you two see that too?"

"Yep. Pretty crazy."

"Pretty awesome, though."

All three had been transfixed by the battle aura that poured
from Alfina. It was vast and far surpassed anything they'd encountered before. A battle aura was a special type of energy that
surrounded everyone, no matter who they were. In times of crisis,
its magnitude increased proportional to an individual's ability.

Emella looked over at Mira, who was still gloating quietly to herself. What were the implications of Mira commanding such a powerful being?

"The summoning techniques you use are formidable," came a voice that was at once familiar and yet entirely alien. "Though this is my first time seeing them, I'd like to talk with you at length once we've achieved our goal and returned to town."

Mira turned and looked at Flicker. Something had changed drastically with the purple-robed mage.

Where was the Flicker who wanted nothing more than to poke and prod and squeal? Instead, the sorceress quietly stared at Mira with inquisitive eyes sparkling like stars in the night sky.

"Emella! Emella! Something's wrong with Flicker!" Mira called, not taking her eyes away from the strange mage.

"What an odd response. We've been together this whole time." Flicker replied as she pushed her glasses back up her nose like an academic interrupted in the middle of a study session.

"Hmm? How so?" Emella snapped from her daze and wandered over to investigate.

"She's gone all...*intellectual*? Whatever it is, it's weirding me out."

"Oh, that's what you meant." Emella smiled mischievously and suddenly hugged the party mage, calling out, "I love you, Flicker!"

"What are you doing? Stop messing around." Flicker brushed off Emella and slipped from her embrace.

Emella stuck out her tongue and laughed. "Just as I expected."

"And? What was that supposed to do?" demanded Mira.

"Now you try it."

"Why would I do such a thing?!" Mira blustered.

"Go on, give it a try, and it will all make sense." Emella grabbed Mira's arms from the back, and like a puppeteer operating an unwieldy marionette, wrapped them around Flicker despite Mira's immediate protest.

"Oof, what are you doing, Emella...aaah?!"

Instantaneously, the composed and intelligent Flicker collapsed like a house of cards as she grabbed Mira and pulled her deeper into the hug, rubbing her face against Mira's soft pudgy cheeks.

"Oh, Mira, did you need some attention? Come here, sweetie, let me give you a hug! I love you too!"

"What have you done?!" cried Mira, angry that she'd ever mentioned the problem in the first place.

"Flicker has a thing for cute girls. Usually, she's calm and calculating—one of the best support mages around—but get her around something adorable in a dress and she can't help herself."

"Couldn't you have just explained that verbally?!" Mira cried desperately as Flicker's wandering hands kept exploring.

"Since this is an afternoon of education, I thought you'd prefer a comprehensive demonstration," Emella responded with a giggle.

"Fool of an elf!"

Mira's scream of anguish echoed through the silence of the catacombs.

The other members of Écarlate Carillon smiled apologetically while Flicker replenished her stores of cuteness at Mira's expense. Tact gave Mira's hand a small squeeze of condolence.

During the five minutes of cuddling, Zephard busied himself by wandering after Alfina to search for loot in her wake. His mastery of stealth made him the perfect candidate for such a task, since if he stumbled across something the Valkyrie had missed, he could simply withdraw from the area unseen.

When he returned, the party moved onward. The long, dark corridor ahead echoed with the sound of Alfina's footsteps and the sounds of metal clashing. Mira tried to keep her Holy Knight between herself and Flicker, wary of the heavy breathing coming from the rear.

As the party made it to the next hall, Mira was the most apprehensive she'd ever been within a dungeon—but they'd encountered no further monsters, just piles of ash scattered about.

"All clear!" shouted Zef, peeking back around the corner with a wave of his hand.

As the group entered, he continued to search the surroundings. Amid the piles of ash, he discovered something glowing.

"Hey, isn't this a Mobility Stone?" he called, picking up a marble-sized purple stone from the ashes.

Asval took the handle of his hammer and used it to scatter another one of the piles. Seeing another Mobility Stone fall out, he raised his lantern and looked around the room. "Are these ashes all that remains of the monsters?"

There were over a dozen piles of ash. Mira reached down to pick up a Mobility Stone from one of them.

Hrmm, looks like loot drops survived the transition.

Mobility Stones were a material item collected primarily from undead monsters. Besides being used by necromancers to animate corpses, they had a number of applications and were always in high demand. Back in the *Ark Earth Online* that Mira knew, players would farm the stones in the catacombs on "grave visits." It was useful to know that the monsters of the catacombs still dropped them after the world had become real.

While Mira was lost in her memories, Zef zipped about to sweep the piles for any hidden Mobility Stones. In the end, the room contained fourteen of the valuable items.

"So this is all thanks to Alfina, right?" he asked as he counted out the loot.

"Based on what we're seeing, that seems to be the case," replied Flicker.

"But how were they all reduced to ash?" he wondered. "Wasn't she carrying a sword? Can she use some form of fire spell?"

It was a fair question, and Flicker pondered for a few moments. "Even with magic, it would take a high-level spell to reduce them to this without leaving other traces. But there's no residual mana in the air, so it couldn't have been sorcery."

As those present considered the discrepancy between the current situation and the facts, their eyes all slid to Mira.

"Go on, then, Mira. Enlighten us," said Zephard with a wry grin.

Spurred on by Zef's prompt and accompanying wink, Mira responded with a haughty "If I must."

"Alfina wields a sword forged from condensed light," Mira proudly explained, finger to her chin. "As it strikes the wicked, it releases a burst of concentrated sunlight...and sunlight incinerates the undead. Nothing here can stop her."

"Such a sword exists...?" Emella stared at one of the ash piles with a twinkle in her eyes. If Flicker had a weakness for cute girls, then the elven warrior had a corresponding vice for nice swords.

"I see. That's rather amazing that you can summon a being wielding such a sword." Much to Mira's delight, Asval's opinion of summoning continued to trend upward.

This raid was progressing more smoothly than Emella had imagined—so much so, it almost couldn't be called a raid at all.

The monsters that normally kept adventurers on guard were all reduced to ash in the path of Mira's minion, leaving Zef to triumphantly sweep through the remains. The only moment that slightly resembled adventure was when the party got turned around in a room with multiple branching passages and Emella had to consult her map.

"Why'd we come down here again? These little guys?" Zef asked, picking yet another Mobility Stone out of the ashes.

The idle comment struck Emella's pride to the core and she could only groan in response. She'd gathered her friends to escort Tact to the Hall of Darkness. It'd seemed to be the only prudent solution at the time. She just couldn't have let a little boy and girl venture off alone into a C-Rank dungeon! Even veterans faced serious danger here. An adult had to step in to make sure they were safe.

But judging from the current state of affairs, Mira alone would have been more than enough to accomplish the deed.

Now Emella was stuck carrying a spirit blade with nothing to swing it at.

"Are we just leeching?" Zef asked.

"Don't say that!" Emella buried her face in her hands.

As the party continued on, they arrived at an atrium midway through the third level. A large pile of ashes sat in the center of the room where the giant ghoul should have been. Zef approached and began kicking through the debris.

"Whoa! A Mobility Crystal!"

Zephard raised the fist-sized gemstone high into the air, and the general mood lifted at once. Mobility crystals were very rare items that could only be obtained from the largest undead monsters. Adventurers had lost their lives trying to secure such treasures.

"Wow! Let me see that!" shouted Emella.

As the reinvigorated vice captain charged at Zef, Asval gazed across the room at the jewel in his hands. "Are you serious?"

"That's a rare find," Mira commented.

Loot secured, the group continued to pick their way through the dungeon until they arrived at their destination on the fifth floor—the Hall of Darkness.

Even at the site of what should have been the most challenging fight in the dungeon, there were no signs of monsters—just scattered piles of ash. The sheer volume of debris was a testament to Alfina's unseen valor, and both Emella and Asval gasped at the sight. According to their plan, it would have been piles of bodies, and they would have borne the brunt of the assault.

"The monsters are defeated," said a voice from one of the side halls as the Valkyrie stepped from the shadows. She showed no signs of exhaustion or damage, and her armor was as pristine as the moment they first saw her.

"Very well done, Alfina. I knew I could count on you."

"I am honored by your praise, Master," the summoned Valkyrie said as she took a knee before Mira.

"Get some rest."

At Mira's words of dismissal, a magic circle appeared to envelop and carry Alfina back to wherever she existed when not summoned by the master of the Tower of Evocation. The rest of the party stood and watched the solemn display, hesitant to interrupt. By the look on Zephard's face, he was disappointed to see her go.

And with that, the dungeon was cleared.

The layout of the fifth level was quite simple. A corridor led from the stairs to a square-shaped hall, and each wall had a door leading to another passageway leading onward. The left passageway led to a storeroom where a chest of loot had once spawned when this was still a game. The path on the far wall led down to the sixth level. All eyes fell on the right-hand passage, which led to Tact's destination.

Emella confirmed this on her map and signaled the party to

follow. Zef, still searching the ashes for treasure, was left to bring up the rear.

"So here we are," Emella said as she reached a copper door at the end of the hallway. She opened it, and they all stepped through.

The party found themselves in a room with an inexplicable language scrawled across the walls. The oddness of the chamber was impossible to ignore, and Mira found her eyes drawn to the full-length mirror on the opposite wall.

Emella and Asval checked for hidden enemies, but there were neither monsters nor piles of ash that might indicate Alfina had been here a few minutes earlier. The only thing of note was the mirror, its oppressive presence magnified by the eerie illumination of lantern light.

While the adventurers looked on in a mixture of apprehension and awe, Mira grumbled to herself and approached the mirror to get on with her mission. Remembering a disastrous quest where the mirror was cursed by a Lesser Demon, she decided to take preventative measures. She reached into her pocket to withdraw a phial of holy water. Popping the cork, she splashed some across the glass and stood back to observe.

"Hrmm, looks all right," she mumbled, then turned and motioned to Tact to come forward.

"Huh? What was that about?" Emella asked with a quirked eyebrow.

"Hm? Oh, just a little...charm," Mira responded evasively, not wanting to go into a story that might blow her cover.

The water slowly dripping from the mirror added to the ee-riness. Though they had reached their target without a scratch, everyone in the room was on edge, save for Mira. Suddenly, the door behind the group flew open and Emella leapt into the air, spinning to reach for her sword.

"Oh, so this is where you guys got to. Did you find the thing?" asked Zephard as he took in the scene.

"W-we found it! See? There it is!" Emella blushed with em-barrassment and pointed to the mirror.

"There you go, Tact. Now you can see your mom and dad again." The rogue clapped a hand to Tact's shoulder as if he'd been the one who made it all possible.

Tears welled in Tact's eyes as he looked around at the party who'd brought him here. "Right! Thank you, thank you all so much!"

"It's easy to use. There are a couple prior conditions that need to be met, such as having a close connection to the departed person you want to contact or having an item of value to them. I think you meet those standards. Now all you have to do is face the mirror and say their names," said Mira, gently patting Tact on the back. "Go on, do your thing, kid."

Taking a step forward he nodded and stood before the mirror. After a moment's hesitation, he conjured fond memories of his mom and dad, then called his parents' names...

...and nothing happened.

"Are they there?" asked Emella, breaking the silence and earn-ing herself a glare from Flicker.

Still, nothing happened.

"Maybe they don't appear to others?" Asval muttered. But no one had an answer for his question, and they all continued to stare at Tact's back.

"Tact."

Mira was the first to notice the change. As the boy's shoulders shook and tears streamed down his face, she ran up and hugged the boy. The other four stepped forward to see what had happened and Tact began to wail while pressing his face into Mira's robes.

"Father... Mother..." he sobbed as Mira gently patted him on the back, catching the endless tears that spilled forth with her clothing.

"What happened? Was it a sad farewell?" she asked.

The boy responded to her questions with a shake of his head. He looked up at her, eyes wet.

"Neither one of them wanted to see me," he managed to get out before breaking down again.

He hadn't been able to see his parents. Both Emella and Flicker wore dispirited expressions as they put their hands on his shoulders. Dismayed and unsure of what to do, Asval opened his Item Box and looked for sweet or a drink that he could offer.

But Zephard stood in front of the Mirror of Darkness, staring at it thoughtfully.

"Lyrica."

His voice was just a whisper, but the name rose up unthinkingly from within like a quiet prayer.

As he said the name, a sliver of light leaked from the dark mirror and a girl—perhaps sixteen years old—slowly appeared within. She wore a red dress, and her brown hair was woven into twin braids. Her eyes gazed at the rogue standing before the mirror with a warm smile.

"It...can't be..."

She was the same age as when she passed away, wearing her favorite dress with her hair done up just as he remembered. His sister looked like she'd just stepped out from his memories.

But he wasn't alone in seeing her; Mira, Emella, and Flicker stood with their eyes glued to the mirror, though they still worked to console Tact.

"Lyrica... Lyrica!" Zephard unthinkingly clutched the mirror and shouted his sister's name.

"Big brother?" The girl in the mirror tilted her head to the side in response.

"Lyrica, I'm sorry," he rasped. "If only I'd come home faster. If only—"

His apologies began to blur together as his voice grew hoarse until he simply began repeating "I'm sorry" over and over again.

"Why are you apologizing? You did nothing wrong." Her words were the only thing that brought pause to Zef's apologies.

"But I...I couldn't save you. If I'd returned to the village sooner, you wouldn't have died." His voice sagged as though he had just confessed a sin.

Asval was the only one among the party who knew the story, and he walked over to Zef with a scowl. But just as he was about to tell Zephard that it never should have fallen upon his shoulders in the first place, Lyrica spoke up again.

"It was the illness that took me, Zef. It wasn't your fault." The girl in the mirror had a bright-red face as she scolded her brother. This wasn't how she remembered him. She didn't want him to apologize or blame himself for such a thing. "Listen to me, Zephard!"

"O-okay!" The anger in Lyrica's voice snapped Zef to attention. As she saw him flinch, she smiled and giggled.

"Wh-what is it, Lyrica?"

"I didn't come here to hear you apologize; I came here to thank you! I'm glad to see you're still the same."

"Huh? Who, me?"

As a child, she'd often have to scold him for losing control of himself. It had been a while since that had happened last, but he'd never forget her chastising.

"It was a plague," she said firmly. "Don't take responsibility for my death, Zef."

"But Lyrica—"

"But nothing! You did all you could to take care of me. And now I can finally tell you—thank you. I love you, Zephard."

As she said this, her form began to slowly fade away. Time was running out.

"Me too. I love you too!" Zef shouted after Lyrica's vanishing shade.

The final image was of a young smiling girl.

She Professed Herself Pupil of the Wise Man

9

WITHOUT ANOTHER WORD, Zephard stepped away from the Mirror of Darkness and turned away from the rest of the party. His tears flowed like Tact's, and he couldn't find the words to speak.

The rest of the party glanced at each other in silent agreement to give their rogue some time alone.

"Looks like the mirror's working fine," Mira said thoughtfully.

"Then what does that mean?" Emella asked, wondering why it hadn't reacted to Tact's call.

"Perhaps it was because he tried for both at the same time?" Flicker hypothesized. "Perhaps the mirror can only summon one shade at a time."

"That's a possibility," Asval said slowly before glancing over at Mira. She nodded and gently positioned Tact in front of the mirror once more.

"Tact, try calling for just your father or your mother this time."

The boy nodded and began to think of his mother. "Mother. Mother Leene!"

Yet the Mirror of Darkness remained silent.

"Father... Ashley!"

Again and again, he implored the mirror and called his parents' names, but no spirit appeared to answer him. His only conclusion was that they had abandoned him, even beyond the grave. Tears welled up in his eyes once more, and the mirror only showed an image of his tear-streaked cheeks and runny nose.

"No one's there," Asval murmured, and Tact broke down into sobs as though his words were the final insult.

As the big man fretted over what he had done, Mira pulled Tact back into her arms and the child's sobbing slowly ceased. But the tears still flowed and he refused to speak.

"What does it all mean?" Emella circled around and around, looking at the mirror, hoping to discover some sort of cause but finding nothing.

"Looks like one at a time didn't do the trick," said Mira sullenly.

"Well, we know it's not broken." Flicker reached out and touched the surface.

Asval stopped panicking and joined her in her inspection, puzzling over the fact that there wasn't even a scratch on it.

The Mirror of Darkness had been a special quest object that allowed users to talk to the dead. Now that the game was reality, it seemed as though it worked regardless of the specific quest, as proven by the situation with Lyrica. But why hadn't Tact's parents appeared? Did they truly not wish to see him?

She immediately dismissed the idea. What sort of parent

wouldn't want to see their child, who obviously cared so much about them?

But what other options could explain its behavior?

Then it dawned on her. "Tact's parents are still alive."

Emella stopped pacing. The whole reason they'd initiated this adventure was to give Tact a chance to reconnect with his departed parents. While Mira's hypothesis made their journey a moot point, it made perfect sense.

"This all started because they were declared deceased after having been missing for the past five years," she said, working through the evidence aloud. "Which means it is possible that they're still alive."

Her expression flipped and she happily ran over to Tact. "Five years missing. Those are just the guild rules. But that doesn't mean that they're actually dead!"

The other three guildmates looked at one another with wide eyes. They only knew that they were escorting a young boy to say farewell to his dead parents, not that they'd been declared dead through stroke of a pen without evidence of their demise.

"Tact." Mira gently released her hold on the boy and looked him in the eyes. Recognizing the seriousness of the situation, he returned her gaze with a sniffle. "I need you to listen very carefully. The Mirror of Darkness is a mirror that reflects the dead. It can't reflect the living. Do you understand, Tact? That means that your parents are still alive."

Alive. The word resounded through his chest, and for a moment, a newfound light banished the darkness that had overwhelmed his spirit. Then he recalled his grandfather's words, and his heart started to sink once more.

"But...Grandpa told me they were dead. He told me to stop hoping."

"But the man from the guild only said they were missing, right?"

"Right."

"You didn't see them pass away, and they can't be reflected in the Mirror of Darkness. Don't you think there's a good chance that they're still among the living?" Mira smiled gently as she finished working him through the logic. "If they're alive, I'm sure you'll see them again."

"Leene and Ashley, was it? If we ever run into them on our travels, we'll tell them all about you, Tact," said Asval as he fought to hold back his own tears.

Flicker removed a small notepad from her pouch and wrote down their names before. "I'm sure they're alive. The fact that they didn't appear in the mirror is proof of that."

"That's right, little man!" exclaimed Zephard, popping back into the conversation, even though his eyes were still a bit red. Banishing any forlorn expression, he smiled as best as he could and looked down at Tact. "Take heart—a kid shouldn't show such despair. I'm sure that your parents would want you to keep smiling. The Écarlate Carillon will find them sooner or later."

"I will, and...and thank you," he replied with the biggest smile they had ever seen. "S-sorry I dragged you all into this, but thank you so much!"

As things began to settle, Mira once again retrieved her phial of holy water and turned to stand in front of the mirror.

"Hey, Howard! Come talk to me. Look! I've got holy water!" Mira shook the phial back and forth, but the mirror remained silent. After waiting a few more moments, she tucked the phial away while mumbling, "Guess that doesn't cut it."

She hadn't really expected to make contact with the old demonologist since they never shared a strong bond. Even though the man loved holy water with a burning fervor, the item was too generic to cause him to respond. It had been worth a shot, but she decided that the best course of action was to report the result back to Solomon and see if he could come up with another idea.

As she spun on her heel away from the mirror, she caught a glimpse of Zef standing alone with a brooding look on his face. Despite Tact being the focus of attention, it seemed like at least one traumatic event of the past had been faced and resolved that afternoon. The sight of him breaking down into tears was a far cry from her first impression of the playboy rogue she'd met that morning in the guild square.

"By the way, Zef...are you doing all right?"

At her question, the rest of the guildmates turned to face Zef, and he flinched at unexpectedly being the new center of attention.

He quickly shook it off, pointed at the ceiling, and declared, "I'm back in action!"

His face was still a little clouded, but that was far more in character with the easygoing Zephard from before. Asval gave him an appraising look, then breathed a small sigh of relief.

Standing on her tiptoes, Mira approached him and reached out toward him.

"Mira, what are you...?"

Just as he asked his question, she patted him on the head.

"I'm glad for you. I don't know the details, but it seems like you found what you needed."

Relief spread through Zephard as though it were his sister comforting him in Mira's place. His mask slipped and his face broke into a natural smile.

"Thank you," he whispered so that only Mira could hear. He allowed himself a moment to indulge in the comfort, then with a gentle chuckle, he softly let the image of his sister he'd conjured up in his mind fade away.

"Well, now that the job is done, I guess it's time to head back," said Emella, clapping her hands to get everyone's attention. "Somewhat unexpected finish...but all's well that ends well, right?"

Zef was seemingly back in fine form; as he turned and looked at the party, his face bore a boyish grin.

"This might be just the beginning for you, Tact."

"Right! I'm going to become an adventurer and go out to find my parents!"

They had to be alive somewhere. The revelation brought Tact much more joy than his original goal would have.

"Speaking of unexpected, what about you, player?" Asval glanced between Zephard and Mira with an arched eyebrow. Their private conversation remained a mystery, but it was obvious the two had shared a moment in the wake of Zephard's revelation at the mirror. "You have a new type now that you've got some closure?"

"What? Did I just hear what I think I heard? I'm sure that was just my imagination!"

"Wait, you knew about that beforehand?" exclaimed Emella. "I had no idea Zef was suffering in silence! I'm supposed to be the vice captain of the guild, and I didn't even recognize that one of my guildmates was so troubled."

Mira smirked at their banter but felt a true joy at the obviousness of the bonds that bound the group together. She was reminded of the old days when the Wise Men were securing a future for Alcait.

Speaking of which...

"Thanks for the help, guys. Would you mind taking Tact back with you? I still have business to attend to on the sixth level."

With Tact's quest concluded, there was no further reason to subject him to the hardships of the dungeon. This party had earned her trust to return him to town safe and sound, and she needed to get on with her mission.

"What business would you have on the sixth level, little miss?" asked Asval suspiciously.

Zephard looked puzzled as well. "I've heard there's nothing down there, just an empty old castle and no monsters."

"That *is* quite odd." Flicker looked at her and pushed up her glasses by wrinkling her nose. "No one has ever reported finding anything on the sixth level."

They weren't wrong. The sixth level was a massive cavern with an underground lake and a huge castle that had been vacant for as long as anyone could remember.

It was unique in that it was the lowest point in the dungeon... and yet nothing was there. Even the interior of the castle was bare, the walls uncovered and lacking any sort of furnishings. There weren't any doors, and what should have been the treasure vault was open and empty.

No treasures, no monsters, and there had never been any special in-game events.

Some of the players who fancied themselves archeologists took interest in the sixth level, but after thoroughly examining every last nook and cranny, they found nothing of interest. It was as if the developers had meant to implement features there but then had gotten sidetracked by more interesting projects.

And somehow, Mira said she had business there.

"That's right. You had the permit for the Ancient Temple before any of this even started," Emella muttered to herself while thinking about the events of yesterday that led them into the dungeon. "I guess the sixth level was your target all along."

Having unexplained business in a place that no one ever went sounded right up Zef's alley. "Well consider me intrigued. I'm going too!"

"I knew it! You *do* have a new type..." Asval laughed.

"I'm telling you, it's not like that!"

"I won't let you have Mira!" cried Flicker, fruitlessly pounding her fists on Zephard's back.

"Please, listen to what I'm trying to say!" shouted Zef as his protests fell on deaf ears. "You all saw how strong she is! I just figured if someone like Mira was getting up to something, it might be worth checking out. No other ulterior motives! None!"

But despite their teasing, the group grew ever more curious. Everyone had heard that nothing was on the sixth floor, but no one had actually seen it for themselves.

So as the group quieted down, Emella presented a collective request from the Écarlate Carillon. "So, Mira, perhaps we could all accompany you?"

"Well, I'm not quite sure what lies ahead, but...suit yourself, I suppose."

She was hoping to find Soul Howl, the Great Wall of Alcait, one of the Nine Wise Men. Mira had always been a bit reluctant to be associated with Soul Howl since his interests had always been a bit...warped. But given the circumstances, she had to acknowledge that the kingdom needed all the help it could get.

Soul Howl might have been a creep, but at least he wasn't an actual psychopath. She counted that as a point in his favor. It was kind of like the difference between going all out on making a tricked-out haunted house and actually hanging corpses from the rafters.

And it was that difference that led Mira to decide that it was probably safe enough for the rest of the party to tag along.

Leaving the Hall of Darkness, she opened the door that led to the sixth level. There were no monsters left to defeat, and it was a straight shot down the corridor to the next level. After walking along the passageway, the party emerged near the top of the underground cavern.

The cave comprised exposed bedrock, but off to the right, a staircase had been gouged out of the rock. It led down the side of the cavern wall to the shore of the lake below. But the size of the steps was inconsistent, and they appeared to be slick and treacherous given the dank nature of the cave.

"Phew, would ya look at that," Zef said, adding a low whistle.

The sixth level was lit by shining crystals, which protruded from the large domed walls, and the whole vastness of the cavern was enveloped in an ethereal light.

"These weren't here the last time I visited," Mira mumbled to herself. "What on earth is he up to?"

She dismissed her light spell and took Tact by the hand, and then she started off down the stairs.

"Th-this is really high up..." Emella turned off her lantern and peered down the stairs hesitantly before plastering herself against the cavern wall to make the descent.

"C'mon, Vice Captain," Asval said with a chuckle as he passed by her. "Cheer up, we're going to get a bit more of that dungeoneering experience."

"I don't know if our illustrious vice captain can handle it." Zephard leered at Emella and then stepped a little closer to the edge as he walked past the swordswoman, continuing down the stairs to catch up with Flicker, who was trying to catch up with Mira in turn.

"Knock it off, Zef!" Emella snapped at the rogue. "You'll get yours sooner or later!"

10

"**Y**OU SHOULD KNOW you brought this on yourself!"

"What did I do to deserve this?!"

As soon as she reached the ground level, Emella turned to attack Zephard with demonic ferocity. He'd spent most of the descent teasing her over what would make any rational person apprehensive, and she was finally on level ground. Now she would have her revenge.

"What a noisy lot." Mira turned from the pair with a bemused look on her face and gazed back out over the giant white castle that sat in the center of the cavern.

If Soul Howl was anywhere in the dungeon, then he would have to be here.

"Let's leave them here and head to the castle," she told the others before stepping off across the bedrock at a brisk pace.

"We're off to the castle!" Asval shouted at the swordswoman and the rogue, who were still tangling with each other by the shore. Based on their shouting, he wasn't sure if they heard him or not.

The path to the castle gate was strewn with scorched rubble. Mira figured it was just remnants of some of Soul Howl's experiments, but she couldn't shake the feeling that she was being watched. She looked around, but aside from her party, no living soul could be found.

"The sight alone makes it worth coming down here," Asval said from right behind her. He gawked up at the grandeur of the castle in between shepherding Tact across some of the more hazardous terrain.

"Indeed," grunted Mira as she passed through the open front gate. If it hadn't been for the fact that it was located in the deepest depths of a dungeon, this castle would no doubt have been a famous tourist attraction. Or at least the perfect roost for bandits in some far-flung mountain range.

A large staircase sat in the center of the entrance hall, and more of the glowing crystals were embedded in the walls. But the walls and floor were bare and unadorned, just as she remembered.

"Now, then, I'll have to insist you all to wait for me here. From this point forward, my business is my own."

Her task to find the Nine Wise Men was a secret order of the king and on a definite need-to-know basis. None of them needed to know what a freak Soul Howl truly was.

Besides, there might have been golems stationed around the castle serving as guards. So long as the others remained in the entrance hall, they shouldn't trigger any response from the security team. Perhaps a living-dead girl would wander through, but no golems.

This all assumed that Soul Howl was here in the first place.

"Hmm, something secret, eh?" Asval couldn't help but be curious, but he found a wall to lean against and signaled that he respected her request.

Flicker was in the same boat, but her comment of "Mira's so mysterious!" implied that her thoughts were trending down a slightly different path.

"Watch over Tact, will you?" Mira said, passing his hand off to Flicker in hopes that a task would keep her from getting carried away.

"You betcha!"

"Stay safe, Miss Mira!" called the boy as she ascended the steps.

"Sure, sure. I'll be right back."

As soon as she was out of sight, Asval picked a corridor and began to make his way deeper into the castle.

"Hey!" protested Flicker. "Mira said her business was a secret!"

"Yeah." Asval paused for a moment. "But her secret is on the second floor. I'm going to stick to the first."

As she ascended to the next floor, Mira began a frantic search for a particular room. Rushing down the corridors and poking her head into each open doorway, she finally found her destination behind a doorless entrance.

"Hrmm... This will have to do," she grumbled.

A hole was positioned in the center of the room—a Japanese-style squat toilet. She lowered her underwear, hiked up her skirt, and squatted down. If she turned her head to the side and craned her neck, she could see all the way down the long hallway and would know instantly if anyone were coming.

Despite the possibly compromising situation, she still let out a sigh of relief.

A moment later, she pulled a square of tissue from her pouch and finished the job. She'd learned her lesson from the poison flower incident and now made it a point to keep some extra toilet paper on hand for emergencies.

With her mind and body restored to harmony, she pulled her underwear back up and activated an ability.

[Immortal Arts: Biometric Scan]

Looks like Emella and Zef have made it to the castle.

She could detect five pings coming from the floor below. But there was no sign of anything coming from above. That said, the sensitivity of the Biometric Scan varied depending on distance and intervening obstacles. The stone walls and sheer size of the castle meant that there was no guarantee she could detect anyone on the higher floors.

And so Mira made her way up to the top floor of the castle to begin her search. As a wizard, she knew that there was nothing a wizard loved more than having private chambers at the top of a tower.

On her way to the top, she considered calling out Soul Howl's name but decided against it, in case she was overheard by the party below. The Nine Wise Men were famed heroes—and if people started asking questions, then the secret part of her secret mission wouldn't be much of a secret anymore.

Instead, she thought about using the nicknames they used to throw about among friends, like Professor Living-Dead Girl, Pervert West: Reanimator, Death of Chivalry, and so on, but those were way too embarrassing to actually say aloud.

It seemed like the fastest way to find him was by searching.

As she arrived on the top floor, Mira immediately used her Biometric Scan to search the surroundings.

"Hrmm, what's this?"

There was a ping right at the edge of her detection range, but it was so small, she could barely pick it up even when focusing directly on the point. She couldn't imagine anyone else would be in a place like this except for the person she was looking for, but the heartbeat she detected was incredibly faint.

With a rising feeling of dread, Mira dropped the spell and moved in the direction of the contact. Her search led to a large hall on the front-facing side of the castle: the throne room.

Mira huddled against the wall outside and cautiously peeked around the corner to check the situation. "What the devil?"

The sight before her was beyond bizarre. With a rueful grin, she proceeded inside.

Countless chairs had been arranged to face the throne dais on the far side of the room, in the manner one might find in a concert hall. Approaching one of the chairs, Mira leaned over to take a closer look at its occupant.

"Suspended animation, eh?" she asked as she touched the cheek of the woman in a maid uniform. It was cold; no warmth of life was present at all. Closed eyes, clenched lips, expressionless—just sitting there.

"His proclivities seem to be advancing in the wrong direction, I'm afraid."

Mira looked about in dismay. On each chair throughout the throne room sat the corpse of a woman dressed in what were unmistakably maid outfits that blended Japanese and Western styles. Each was perfectly embalmed in a manner that caused them to appear as if they were simply having a rest. While it was a bit more extreme than she remembered, she had a strong hunch that this was the work of Soul Howl.

But these bodies wouldn't have caused a reaction on her Biometric Scan. As a sanity check, she refocused her attention.

The ping was coming from the direction of the dais—and upon closer inspection, one body clearly stood out from the rest. There were two thrones on the platform, and one was occupied by the only body in the room not dressed in a maid uniform.

Perhaps seventeen or eighteen years old, she was beautiful, with delicate eyes and a petite nose. Her indigo hair fell over her shoulder and flowed down below her waist. The color contrasted sharply with her flawless, pallid skin. With closed eyes, her face wore a joyless smile.

More importantly, and unlike the rest of the occupants of the room, she was the source of the meager heartbeat that Mira had discovered earlier. Approaching the throne, Mira reached out to touch the girl's neck and check for any vital signs.

"She's frozen..." Mira's hand recoiled from her skin, which was as cold as ice. Mira needed answers. "Soul Howl! Are you here?!"

After waiting for ten, then twenty seconds, she received no response. It looked like she would have to find her own clues to solve this mystery.

Poking around the room, she found a door behind the dais leading to an antechamber. With papers and books scattered across the room, it seemed like a promising place to start. A desk was stacked with reference texts and ancient documents, countless scribbles in their margins.

Mira traced her fingers across the poor handwriting, trying to make sense of the penmanship.

"The *Holy Grail of Heavenly Light*...?" The phrase appeared over and over again, and she recognized the name of the item.

The Holy Grail of Heavenly Light was legendary in every sense. It was said to remove any condition, heal any wound, repel any monster, turn aside death, nullify penalties after losing a battle, and provide the absolute defense and offense against the archenemy of all mankind—demons.

But while other legendary items had been obtained by players over the years, no one had ever managed to secure the Holy Grail. Players didn't know if it was a monster drop, something that could be crafted, or nestled in a dungeon somewhere. Most assumed that it had never been implemented in game and that it was just residual metadata.

But why was he doing all this research into it?

For the Nine Wise Men, few problems couldn't be solved through the development of new techniques. The Grail was powerful, certainly, but nearly all of its properties could be replicated through other means. So then, why?

As she pondered, the image of the frozen lady from the throne room popped into her head.

Leaving the antechamber, Mira returned to inspect the woman on the throne. She felt a bit like a degenerate poking and prodding at the girl, but she consoled herself by affirming that this was a clinical examination and in the service of king and country—most certainly not some carnal pastime. She wasn't some weirdo like Soul Howl.

"Hrmm, nothing..." Her impromptu exam at an end, Mira carefully smoothed out the dress to its original state and stepped away from the girl to allow herself a full-body view. Everything about the situation was so abnormal, it was hard to find any one thing that stood out.

But as she stared at the figure, Mira realized there was one place she hadn't checked. Because of how the woman was seated, her back had remained concealed the entire time.

Slowly and carefully, Mira eased the woman forward so she could have a look. The back panel of the dress was cut open revealing flawless skin—which was oozing sickeningly dark blood and etched with a hexagram.

Mira had seen this before.

Symbols and shapes lined the perimeter of the hexagram, and the letters "XV" were engraved in the center. The strange markings were a seal called the Curse of the Underworld, or sometimes a Demon's Blessing. The marking spelled certain doom for the bearer.

There had been an event called "Shadow of Black Wings," and Mira remembered it well for its bitter ending. Players were tasked with saving a knight who had been branded with the seal, but despite their efforts, the knight perished.

That memory in turn led her to think of the Holy Grail of Heavenly Light. It was true that almost no technique was beyond the capability of a motivated Wise Man, but in this case, the Grail was warranted. Soul Howl must be a man on a mission.

She turned her attention back to the girl. She was ice-cold, but the fact that she caused a response to the Biometric Scan indicated that she was still alive.

Alive, yet frozen.

Mira didn't remember a technique that could achieve such a result, but she recalled some of the documents she'd rifled through a moment earlier. Alongside information regarding the Grail, there were a great number of necromantic texts and grimoires. Soul Howl must have developed a technique to slow the progression of the curse. Only then had he left the castle in search of the Grail, she surmised.

"All for a living girl. Looks like his proclivities actually swung in the other direction after all." With a wry smile, Mira bowed to the woman on the throne in a brief show of thanks before leaving the room.

Her mission wasn't a failure, but it certainly wasn't over.

While the Ancient Temple was a bust, Mira had found traces of Soul Howl's presence. That said, if he was out searching for as legendary an item such as the Holy Grail of Heavenly Light, her task just became a lot more complex.

Mira wandered around the castle, collecting anything that might give her a hint as to where he'd gone.

"Oho, now this is good." While searching his rooms to collect documents containing records of experiments and thoughts on necromancy, she stumbled across his wardrobe.

They may have disagreed on their taste in women, but Danblf and Soul Howl had always shared a taste in fashion. The stone room had a full-length mirror along one wall and hanger racks lined with robes along the other. Mira's eyes sparkled at the colors and fits, and she was sure she could find something that caught her fancy.

"I'm sure he won't mind me borrowing one or two," she muttered, making excuses to no one in particular as she began rummaging through the clothes.

She'd return them when she finally found the errant necromancer, but until then, he certainly wasn't getting any use out of them. Besides, she didn't particularly want to spend the rest of her life in outfits handpicked by the palace maids. The sooner she was back in clothes suited to her own tastes, the happier she would be.

Stripping off her gothic lolita ensemble, she began pulling stacks of robes from the rack to try on. Unfortunately, none of them fit, and her despair only grew with each attempt. Finally, she happened across a collection of short robes, cut in a way that they didn't seem too unwieldy if she rolled the sleeves up a little.

"Hrmm... But this just emphasizes how adorable I am."

She looked at herself in the mirror, fluttering a hem that made a joke of modesty as she admired her own physical charm.

Most robes occupied both the chest and legs slot in the equipment screen, but short robes were an item that required a matched top and bottom. On its own, it was practically just a miniskirt dress.

As she tried walking about, it revealed flashes of her underwear—a cheap thrill in an abandoned castle, but nothing she'd be seen walking down the streets of Karanak in. Mira reluctantly gave up on her attempt to raid Soul Howl's wardrobe.

Dressed once more, she made her way back to the first floor of the castle, where the rest of the party was waiting. In the entrance hall, she found Emella and Flicker huddled together with ashen faces. Asval looked a bit pale as well, but Zef and Tact were playing a game of cards in the corner. The rogue waved as he noticed Mira coming down the stairs.

"What's the matter with you lot?"

Emella and Flicker just stared at her blankly.

"Is everything all right?" She turned away from the pair's nervous stares just in time to catch Tact as he jumped toward her.

"Welcome back, Miss Mira!" he exclaimed with a carefree smile.

"Were you well behaved for everyone?"

"Yeah!" Tact responded with an earnest nod.

Mira patted him on the head, "That's good to hear."

"Mira...what *is* this place? I thought there wasn't supposed to be anything here," Emella said in a voice so soft that it was almost a whisper.

"What? Did something happen?"

"Dead maids. Dead maids everywhere..." Flicker mumbled.

Everything began to fall into place. Emella and the others must have found bodies like the ones that were in the throne room—a lot of them. To the casual observer, Soul Howl's work probably seemed like that of a madman. Unless they knew the circumstances, it would have been a veritable horror show.

"Don't worry, it's just a bit of necromancy."

Emella tilted her head to the side. "Necromancy?"

"Are you saying there's a necromancer in here?" Asval said, exhausted. He sat down with a heavy sigh and stared straight at Mira.

"There *was* a necromancer in here. But it looks like he's gone somewhere else for the time being."

"And from how you're talking, I'm assuming you had some sort of business regarding that necromancer?"

"More or less. Nothing you need to worry about. He's got strange hobbies...but he's not a bad guy."

The others looked skeptical.

Necromancy wasn't really the art of manipulating corpses so much as it was the art of manipulating souls. Those souls were a form of pure positive energy that necromancers would place into bodies, be they dead or artificial.

It was also formally ranked as one of the nine major schools of magic. As such, it wasn't seen as taboo, even if most people still regarded the practice as being a little creepy. Its adherents weren't considered normal by any stretch of the imagination.

Emella, Flicker, and Asval weren't happy about the situation, but they didn't seem inclined to ask any more questions once necromancy entered the conversation. Zephard, on the other hand...

"Necromancy, huh? I wonder what you could do with that." He was half-joking, his will shaken by the scores of beautiful maids.

STILL RATTLED, Emella found herself jumping and flinching at even the slightest noise. Asval was faring a little better, but he still looked uncomfortable and seemed ready to leave the castle as soon as possible.

As a mage, Flicker lost all trace of anxiety when she learned that one of the major disciplines was at work. Having the opportunity to fawn over Mira once again didn't hurt either.

"Hey, why don't we have some food? I worked up an appetite getting all the way down here," Zef said, plopping to the ground and rubbing his stomach.

"Hrmm, indeed," Mira agreed, feeling pangs of hunger as well. The other guild members nodded halfheartedly and began pulling ingredients and cooking utensils from their Item Boxes.

"Come on, you too, Vice Captain." Zephard prodded Emella.

"I'm good, thanks."

The men were in charge of the cooking while the women were in charge of supplying the ingredients, which allowed the ladies to sit around and chat while the food was prepared.

"By the way, about earlier," said Emella, trying to take her mind off of what she'd stumbled across in the castle. "Who was that guy you called for at the mirror? Howard, wasn't it? Or is that also a secret?"

"Oh, did I pique your interest?" Mira replied as she passed Tact an apple au lait.

"Well, there's a possibility that I might have met him before, I think."

Mira stared at Emella for a moment and considered her reply. Her reasons for finding Howard were still confidential, and she didn't feel like spreading rumors about the threat of encroaching demons. At the same time, Howard had been a fairly well-known character, and there was a chance she could find someone who *did* have a connection with him that would be strong enough to call him in the mirror. Besides, perhaps the Howard whom Emella knew was a different person. Mira wasn't expecting much, but figured she'd start with a few easy-to-recognize features.

"He called himself a demonologist and always wore this trench coat and capotain hat."

"I knew it! That's the same old Howard I met!" Emella's expression brightened and her eyes narrowed as she reminisced.

"What gave it away?"

"Oh, it had to be him. A while back, in the Lion King's Lair, he popped out of nowhere and splashed me with holy water. When I saw you sprinkling holy water on the mirror and saying his name, he was the first thing that came to mind."

"He got you too, huh..." Mira and Emella shared a bitter smile at the recollection.

Sprinkling someone with holy water was the first step in an exorcism when checking if someone was under demonic influence. For Howard, it was just a standard greeting.

"So, why did you want to talk with old man Howard? Could it...have something to do with the stories we've heard lately about Lesser Demon incursions?" Emella lowered her voice and crawled closer to Mira.

"Well, I can't say that it doesn't." Mira scooted away, not liking the sudden turn in the conversation.

It was no surprise that the news of the demon incursions had begun to spread. When half the Alcaitian army was called out to deal with the threat, there was no way to keep it under wraps. Still, her own association with the king needed to be downplayed so she could slip easily into other countries should the need arise.

"I knew it," said Emella with a joyless grin. "I've heard nothing but bad things about them, and the other day, our guild got word that they had started appearing again. I've been trying to find out more."

"They say they've also been showing up around Alcait recently," Flicker interrupted, having somehow tucked herself so that Mira scooted into her as she tried to scoot away from Emella.

Mira tensed for a moment, but Flicker didn't seem to push her luck. Maybe she was in her intellectual state again...maybe she'd learned her lesson.

As she relaxed, she couldn't help but focus on some of the things that they said. *Again*? *Also around Alcait*? It sounded like there had been more appearances of the demons than just the ones she'd been involved in.

"I know about the incidents near Lunatic Lake. Have there been others?"

"Sure enough," Flicker smiled and leaned in as she eagerly began to elucidate.

Word had traveled among the top guilds that two other kingdoms were also attacked by packs of monsters being led by Lesser Demons. Their motives were currently under investigation, but a general warning to nearby adventurers would be issued soon enough. Mira was impressed by the speed of the work being done to mobilize the guilds in response to an emerging crisis.

After listening to Flicker's story, Mira put a finger to her chin and groaned as she pondered over the details. It seemed the issue of invading monster hordes wasn't just limited to the Kingdom of Alcait and was far more of a threat than the in-game events she was used to. It seemed several player-founded nations had been attacked and managed to bring the situation under control while minimizing loss of human life...so far.

Nothing was preventing future incursions by Lesser Demons. But what were they after? What did all of these incidents have in common?

Looking for links between the wealth of information, Mira sank her consciousness into the sea of wisdom. Flicker took the opportunity to sneak up to her side, staring at her with glittering eyes.

"Your serious expression is so cute!" She let out a sigh and lunged forward, only to be struck down on the fly by one of Emella's knife-hand chops.

Unaware of the momentary battle that had occurred, Mira was lost in the memories of past quests involving Lesser Demons. The motives of the Lesser Demons had always been shrouded in mystery, even back during the game. The only common thread between the in-game events were their inevitable pyrrhic conclusions. But this new wave of outbreaks—with coordinated incursions in multiple locations—was clearly the start of something larger.

This just keeps getting more intriguing and troubling.

Now she lamented that she hadn't gotten the chance to talk to Howard. He may have been a self-educated demonologist, but his information was solid, and he probably would have had some sort of hint as to what was going on. Mira frowned and sighed before glancing over in Emella's direction.

"I don't suppose you had a deep connection with Howard? One that might be able to call him in the mirror?"

Typically, in order to use the mirror, you had to have some kind of strong bond with the person you wished to see—for instance, you might be their blood relative, a lover, or a best friend. Mira had only ever interacted with him through quests, so that wouldn't cut it.

Emella shook her head with an apologetic smile. "Probably not. I only met him that one time in the Lion King's Lair, and I doubt that would be enough."

"But the mirror doesn't require that the person have a *connection*, just an item with a strong link to the dead, right?" Flicker said quietly with an intellectual-looking smile as she slowly got to her feet. It seems her cuteness lust had subsided. "Why don't we try our luck in Iblis Village? That's where Howard did his final research. Maybe he left something behind."

"Iblis Village, hmm? Kind of a hike but possibly worth it." Mira rubbed her chin. Maybe she could convince Solomon to send someone to collect his leftover possessions.

As Mira began to ponder the logistics, Flicker's affliction surged back with a vengeance.

"Mira's so cute!"

And once again the purple-clad mage was felled by Emella's hand before Mira could even notice.

12

THE LUNCH PREPARED by Asval and Zef was so fine that it wouldn't have been out of place if served in a fancy restaurant. Completely satisfied, Mira sipped her after-meal tea and sighed, her face the picture of contentment.

"You know what? This place is actually pretty nice. Even for a dungeon," Zef muttered as he lay back and stared at the ceiling.

"Oh, that's right, we're still in a dungeon," said Flicker absently.

Asval rolled his eyes. "Oof, I almost forgot."

Mira drained the last of her tea and tucked her dishes back into her Item Box. Then she rose to her feet and stretched her back.

"Well now, with everything taken care of, I suppose it's time we head back."

This portion of her mission was done. She'd come to the Ancient Temple to search for the whereabouts of Soul Howl and she was leaving empty-handed, save for some clues as to where he might have gone. Her business concluded, she quickly began preparations to depart.

"Yes, let's," said Emella, clearing away her own dishes and strapping her sword back to her waist. "No matter how safe this may seem, we are still in the deepest reaches of a dungeon, after all."

"All right."

"Good point. Let's be off."

"We're outta here!"

The other members of the guild voiced their agreement as they climbed to their feet and lightly stretched themselves in preparation for the long climb back to the entrance. Tact quickly reclaimed his position at Mira's side.

With everyone ready, the group left the giant white castle and headed across the rugged terrain to the stairs leading to the upper levels. The even lighting of the crystals was eerie, leaving no shadows on the ground as they journeyed forth.

"Wait, is there something out there?" Zef said as he stopped and stared out toward the lake.

The smooth, circular shape of the lake made it look as if someone had taken a massive spoon and scooped out the bedrock. Its surface glistened and sparkled in the glow of the crystals, and a faint luminescence could be seen just beneath the surface of the water.

"You're seeing things," Asval replied as he squinted toward the water. "There aren't any monsters down here, and even the most curious adventurers don't bother coming down this far. It's just the shimmer playing tricks in the corner of your eye."

"Hrmm, Zef's correct. We're not alone." Mira searched the area with her Biometric Scan and something pinged on her radar.

She moved to shield Tact with her body. "Don't know what it is, but it's big and it's in the lake."

Asval pulled his hammer from his back with a weary sigh. "Gimme a break! What the heck would even be down here?!"

"That's right, there shouldn't be any monsters on this level," said Emella as she readied her sword.

A moment later, the lake's surface began to ripple. The party tensed at the strange undulations and readied themselves for battle. Whatever it was, they had to deal with it now. If it surfaced after they started up the stairs, there would be no way to fight it in a coordinated manner.

A column of water burst from the lake accompanied by a roar of noise. The spray refracted the light of the crystals and from within a pitch-black shadow emerged to leap forth and land before the party.

"What the heck?!" blurted Asval.

"What's...what's that doing here?!" Emella cried out.

It was entirely black. Though it had a humanoid shape, its form was unnatural and swollen. Claws jutted from the tips of its fingers, and it clicked them together as it peered at them through slit-pupil eyes. It lacked a nose, two twisted horns arose from its head, and bat-like wings sprouted from its back.

It looked just like the beings that had plunged the world into chaos only ten years earlier.

"Oh hell, it's a demon..." muttered Zephard.

"I thought they were wiped out..." Flicker stared wide-eyed at the alien creature standing before them.

"What's a demon doing in this place?" Mira wondered aloud.

Quickly summoning a Holy Knight, she ordered it to protect Tact without taking her eyes off the monster. Giving the boy a light shove in the opposite direction, she ordered, "Go, hide yourself in the castle."

Taking a last look at the demon, Tact nodded and fled, with the Holy Knight following close behind.

Demons. The archenemy of mankind. The ten years prior, the Defense of the Three Great Kingdoms had been an all-out war for survival between humanity and the demon-led forces of monsters. At great cost, humanity had triumphed and the demons were destroyed.

Yet the being before them was unmistakably a demon.

A vision of the woman in the castle throne room rose in Mira's mind. Perhaps this was the cause of her plight. With no way to ascertain the particulars of the marking on her back, she couldn't be sure—but there was little doubt that they were in a fight for their lives, here and now.

"To think I'd find anyone in a place like this." The demon's voice was distorted, as though it were speaking underwater. A massive scythe appeared in its hands. "What luck! You'll make fine offerings."

"Looks like there's only one way out of this," Zef said uneasily as he drew his daggers and crouched low.

The rest of the party readied themselves as well. Emella and Asval braced against surprise strikes, crouching low to prepare for an attack. Flicker withdrew her deck of cards and made ready to cast.

Mira warily kept watch over the beast and pondered her next move. A demon on the sixth floor of the Ancient Temple was unheard of—but observing your enemy was the first step in defeating your enemy. This called for use of Inspect.

"Hrmm... A third-rank count? Well, now, do you think you'll be able to handle us?"

"A count?" Asval had faced demons before. When he'd first become an adventurer, black clouds had covered the sky and swarms of demons poured forth. He still recalled the memories vividly. So many adventurers were overrun, including those he'd looked up to. Was he stronger now than they had been then?

He shook his head to dispel his own doubts. There was no avoiding this.

"We can't take something like this head-on unless we're willing to make sacrifices," Asval said painfully as he stared at the creature, the memories of the heroes who had destroyed the attacking demons filling his mind.

Back in the game, a lowly third-rank baron was more than a match for a rookie player. The hierarchy of demons had baron at the bottom, then viscount, and then count. Assuming the level of difficulty hadn't changed, an opponent of this strength would have required at least six top-level players.

Or one Wise Man.

"Hrmm, very well, then." Mira glanced between the pained expressions of Asval and Emella. It was clear that the members of Écarlate Carillon recognized the difficulty of this foe.

I haven't really had a chance to test my limits since arriving in this world...

Many years before, she'd defeated a third-rank duke—but that was in-game with proper equipment and plenty of restoratives. Now she had to contend with the consequences of the world being real, amplified by the fact that she'd given some of her best gear to Cleos.

Her anxiety was building. She hadn't experienced proper combat in this world and wasn't prepared to risk her own life. She'd been hoping to gradually acclimate to this new reality, but now it seemed that she'd been tossed into the deep end. How far could she push this new body?

But everything she knew—her experience, skills, and knowledge—stemmed from the world as a game. Based on that, the demon before her was no match for a member of the Nine Wise Men.

"Stand back. I'll take care of him," she declared, her voice low, as she stepped forward alongside Asval and Emella.

She'd only known them for a short while, but there was no doubt in her mind that her party members were fundamentally good people. She could protect them. Her decision was made.

"But it's a demon! No matter how strong you might be, you just can't!" Emella gasped, not taking her eyes from their foe.

"Call Alfina! I know it takes time to summon her...but we can buy you that time." Asval gripped his hammer and made a probing lunge at the enemy.

Mira didn't spare them a glance. Instead, she summoned a Dark Knight before her, and her minion hit the ground running.

"We don't have time for that!" she shouted over the high-pitched sound of clashing metal.

Echoes and shockwaves of the Dark Knight's collision with the demon rippled through the air. Her summoned spirit turned aside the destructive power of the demon's scythe with its greatsword.

"How?!" Cold sweat trickled down Asval's forehead.

Emella was unable to react—all she could do was point her sword toward the demon and watch. The clash served as an illustration of the beast's power.

"All of you, fall back!" Mira shouted to the members of Écarlate Carillon.

"But we can't just..." Emella began, turning to look at Asval out of the corner of her eye.

Mira might be a powerful summoner, but how could they leave this battle resting solely on the shoulders of a child? Yet the demon's clash with the Dark Knight left no doubt in their mind that they were hopelessly outclassed in this fight. The best they could do would simply serve as a momentary distraction.

Voices rang out behind them.

"Come on, you two, back to the castle!"

"Yeah! That's our best option!"

Turning, they saw Flicker and Zef desperately gesturing at them to run.

Just as they were about to protest, Flicker continued, "Mira can't use her full power if you're in the way!"

As a mage, Flicker could see the magical power of the demon enveloping it like a ghostly shroud, but she could also see Mira's power growing and threatening to overwhelm the dark force.

"Sorry, little miss! We're leaving this to you!" called Asval.

"Mira, if it gets too dangerous—run for it! We'll find some way to hold it off!" insisted Emella as she began to back away.

Exchanging a glance, the two warriors fell back. Mira didn't speak, but simply gave a nod and a bold smirk.

Taking one more look back as they ran, Asval saw the image of a legendary hero superimposed over the girl's small figure.

"It can't be," he muttered, certain that it was just the stress of the situation getting to him.

"Ha! You friends have abandoned you, human. You are powerful, but your struggle will be in vain," said the demon as he forced the Dark Knight back with the sound of shearing metal. "Introductions are in order, I believe. I am Wolf Bane, Soultaker of Valnares."

The demon finished his introduction by offering a polite bow. Demon he may be, but Wolf Bane bore the rank of count and carried the pride of nobility. His wickedness was wrapped in a warped mockery of courtesy.

"I'm Mira, a summoner, as you can see." She gestured to the Dark Knight, then sketched a slight bow of her own.

"Heh heh heh. A summoner? Then I need only destroy your armor spirit to end this little skirmish."

With that, he leapt into the air and swung a blow with all his might, combining his strength and gravity to bring his weapon down upon the Dark Knight. Amid the tortured clash of metal on metal was the sound of the rock beneath the spirit's feet crumbling and caving in.

Using its sword to block the blow, the Dark Knight proved stronger than the earth beneath it—but as the ground gave way, the summoned spirit lost its footing, and Wolf Bane didn't waste the opportunity.

The moment his feet hit the ground, he twisted his upper body and swung his scythe sideways with immense force. The blade sang through the air, then bit deep into the side of the off-balance armor spirit. The demon's power and the concussive force of the blow sent the Dark Knight flying.

"Now your knight in shining armor is no more, little princess!" Wolf Bane's face contorted in pleasure as he turned and targeted Mira with a downward strike.

But the black blade pierced nothing but stone. The girl who had been there only moments before had vanished, leaving only an illusion in her stead.

"Where did she...?!"

[Immortal Arts, Heaven: Refined Thrust]

From the demon's blind spot, Mira slipped in close and pummeled it using one of her immortal techniques. The layered shockwaves crashed into the unwary demon like a raging tempest.

Hrmm... That seemed to do a little damage. Mira watched Wolf Bane's distorted face as he flew through the air before slamming into the bedrock.

Keeping the demon in sight, Mira lightly flexed her hands to check the feedback from the attack. Based on what she'd felt from her fists, there was almost no difference in the feeling of combat from when she fought using her VR rig.

There *was* a difference in reach—but that was more the result of inhabiting a smaller body than Danblf's. She quickly found she could compensate for that with an extra half-step forward. As a bonus, the smaller body made it easier to slip inside her foe's guard. One touch had allowed her to analyze so much.

Another worrying factor was the physical difference that came with being real instead of virtual. Air resistance and actual gravity governed the laws of nature instead of a computer's physics engine. But given the success of her first strike, the changes seemed minute, and she was adjusting with every passing second.

But not every difference was a hindrance—her senses were clearer, and she could *feel* what was around her. The intuitive flow of her whole body allowed her to be much more responsive.

The fundamental basis for Mira's strength was her accumulated experience and her ability to combine her various acquired skills on the fly. Power In *Ark Earth Online* had ultimately resided in the imagination and skill of the player rather than a random number generator, and as she squared off against the demon, she found that not much had changed.

A brand-new player with prior martial arts or swordsmanship experience was often able to defeat mid-level monsters or oppose player characters using just that physical knowledge. Which meant that to become stronger, players not only had to improve their skills within the system but also in real life.

One player, Kenoh Kojiro the Fist, was famous for fighting monsters in hand-to-hand combat before going on to win national karate tournaments. They stopped only when their body reached its limits. With her abilities in close combat as a Sage of the immortal arts, Mira could pass for a world-class martial artist when it came to skill.

With discipline and practice, you too might be able to fight demons one day.

Wolf Bane rose from the bedrock, brushing off crushed stone and dust as he stood. He glared at Mira. "Damn you! What was that?!"

"Just a little tap. Was it too much for you?"

Mira sucked in a series of deep breaths as she expanded her consciousness, remembering who she had been in the game and applying it to the present. She could feel Danblf's power still flowing through her, and she smiled. The pleasant tingle of the excitement of battle was nostalgic and welcome.

"Don't get cocky, girl!"

Her smile stoked Wolf Bane's fury, and red flames billowed from the scythe in his hands as his anger grew. Raising the weapon, the demon lunged forward, and the fires roared as he slashed at her.

Mira dodged to the side with a flash of footwork, but the demon twisted to strike at her again. Yet she was no more than an illusion, and Wolf Bane slid across the ground with another resounding thud.

Mira gave a little smirk. "I should thank you. You've helped me regain my form."

The demon stormed forward and she met him with more illusions. At the onset of the fight, her movements had been large and overly evasive, but with each exchange, they grew more refined.

Now she was operating from pure muscle memory. As the demon attacked again, she slipped by the scythe by a paper-thin margin, juking inside of the foul count's reach and thrusting her fist into Wolf Bane's stomach.

"You think you're so clever!" he screamed as he doubled over in pain.

After countless such pokes and prods, the demon flew into a rage. He was at the mercy of a little girl! For a noble of his pedigree, the situation was insufferable.

The scythe whined as he placed his full weight into the next strike, but Mira easily avoided it. Crimson flames seared the ground as his attack went wide, and Mira turned to go on the offensive.

Seizing the momentum, she spun around and kicked the back of one of the demon's knees, where his thick, black hide was the weakest. As he crumpled from the blow, she ran up his back and placed her right hand between the horns on his head.

[Immortal Arts Earth: Crimson Bouquet]

Her palm glowed red as she concentrated her will, and a directional blast of flame burst forth onto the demon's scalp.

"Gaah!" Wolf Bane tumbled across the ground, cradling his scorched head in his hands as he staggered back to his feet. His eyes were filled with an insane fury.

"Hrmm... Looks like special techniques are the way to go."

All of Mira's many prior strikes had hurt the demon, but Wolf Bane's tough hide left him largely uninjured and her knuckles sore and red. That didn't surprise her—her current physical abilities weren't too far off from a standard mage, since she'd given Cleos her equipment that'd strengthened her constitution.

Most of the immortal arts were affected by a player's physical stats. She could compensate for that with her high magical ability, but her lack of strength still resulted in lower attack power.

The true battle style for practitioners of the immortal arts was a blend between physical strikes and wizardry. For most opponents, martial arts were sufficient to ensure victory, but it looked like Mira was going to have to lean on the more mystical aspect of her second class to see this battle through.

[Immortal Hidden Arts: True Sight]

Lightly closing her eyes, Mira focused her senses as she had when she was Danblf. As her eyelids slowly opened, they revealed pupils dyed as blue as the midday sky. The buff increased all her abilities and strengthened any other immortal art technique she might choose to use.

The spike in magical power was visible to Flicker, who was watching the battle from a castle balcony. The vast rush of power almost threatened to swallow her own consciousness as the pressure wave nearly knocked her off her feet.

"What's wrong, Flicker?" Emella asked, reaching out to steady her guildmate.

"Something about Mira changed. She's gotten stronger...more *intense*." Wobbling as she stood back up, she stared out at Mira. The rest of the party shuffled nervously and made sure they had a clear line of retreat into the stone building. Just in case...

The battle between Mira and the demon shifted into a new phase. Having regained his wits enough to stop lashing out randomly at Mira's many illusions, Wolf Bane wreathed his hands in black flame and went on the offensive once more.

As Mira dodged a downward swing of his weapon, the black flames continued to chase her and pressed the attack.

[Immortal Arts Earth: Enveloping Gale]

Cool winds enveloped her body, driving away the chasing flames. She took the opportunity to dart inside the demon's guard and drove the heel of her palm into a spot just below his ribs. The power of the winds coiled around her hand, creating a vacuum at their epicenter and a high-speed vortex orbiting her fist.

"Hrng!" he grunted, staggering back.

Despite the pain, he mustered his strength and took a large step forward, swiping upward with his scythe. Even the force of her wind couldn't deflect it. The heat of the flame in its wake forced Mira to step back. The demon followed through by thrusting his off hand forward, to chase her back with a fist full of black fire.

"Oho! Not bad, lowlife!" Dispelling the wind and crossing her arms, Mira fixed Wolf Bane with her shining blue eyes.

"You dare mock me, little girl?!" With a shout of rage, his magical power intensified. The black flames grew, climbing up his arms to cover his entire body before erupting up toward the roof of the cavern. "If you won't submit, I'll burn this whole place down!"

The blaze collapsed, wrapping around the demon, and Wolf Bane—now a jet-black sun—roared and shot forward like a cannonball.

"Witness your doom!"

His scythe glowed from the intense heat of the black flame. Thanks to Mira's True Sight, she saw the upward swing racing toward her, shattering the earth beneath it.

"Not today!" In the same moment, she used both her Immortal Arts: Refined Thrust and Immortal Arts, Movement: Shrinking Earth to close the gap between her and the demon in an instant.

Her speed caused the air in her path to condense into a shock-wave as she flew forward, piercing the black flame and slowing the demon's momentum. The sudden hole in his defenses opened up an inviting opportunity.

"What...?!" he screamed as she launched another Immortal Arts: Refined Thrust at point-blank range.

Wolf Bane flew into the air, scattering his black flames—but despite the pain, he somehow managed to spread his wings and hover above the battlefield. The toughness of the demon's hide was not to be underestimated.

"Damn you, child! What will it take to end you?!" Confident in his safety aloft, the demon gritted his teeth and bitterly weighed his next move.

[Immortal Arts, Earth: Raging Strike]

A series of shockwaves erupted from Mira's palm, growing to an unstoppable crescendo before crashing into the flying demon. The fury blew Wolf Bane back, and he smacked into the uneven stone below, unable to stay airborne. Amid the sound of shattering stone, Mira advanced with her eyes fixated on the demon crawling from the rubble.

"I never thought I'd find a human as skilled as you."

Even after taking point-blank hits from immortal techniques, the demonic count still wasn't showing much sign of injury.

"And I didn't think demons came as tough as you," Mira grumbled as she kept the demon in her sight.

"I feel nothing!" he roared. "My body is too strong for your feeble attacks!"

"You've been a good opponent," Mira said. "But it's time to end this."

[Forbidden Immortal Arts: Unsealed Demon's Eye]

Her right eye darkened while the pupil began to emit a golden glow, gleaming like an evil moon in a pitch-black sky. Pierced by her stare, Wolf Bane was overcome with fear and trembled uncontrollably at the predatory aura rolling off the girl in waves.

[Forbidden Immortal Arts: Paralyzing Demon's Gaze]

He tried to point his flame-cloaked scythe back toward the ceiling. But a moment later, the weapon slipped from his hand as he lost control of his grip.

"What...ugh...paralysis?!" he shrieked. "Such impudence! You cheat, you cheat!"

The technique immobilized foes caught in the gaze of the

Demon's Eye and would begin to destroy them from within—so long as Mira could hold her target within her vision for long enough. Thankfully, Wolf Bane's fall from the air had caused him to land slightly farther away, giving her a wider field of view.

"No... Nooooooo!" Wolf Bane shouted as he fought the paralysis.

First fingers, then arms, then his shoulders slowly broke free. Mira knew that demons were highly resistant to status effects, and the only reason the paralysis had worked even for a short time was due to her overwhelming magical ability.

"I should've known it wouldn't hold a demon for long," she said.

But a short time was all she needed.

She'd been able to overpower Wolf Bane, knocking him down time and time again—but the demon's iron constitution proved to be a problem. She could hold him at bay, but her Sage arts would take forever to whittle away at his defenses.

"Time to wrap this up."

The moment she spoke, the demon's body froze—not from her paralyzing gaze but from the sudden presence that appeared just behind him. He reflexively tried to turn, but his movement was still slowed, and his eyes went wide as a jet-black blade pierced through his chest.

"Guh...ohhh... It can't be..." Choking on the dark blood that filled his mouth, he continued to fight to turn around with his face showing astonishment.

Behind him were the flickering red eyes of the Dark Knight, still active and still deadly.

While fists may not have been an effective weapon against a demon of this caliber, the keen blade of Mira's spirit was up to the task. All it needed was a distraction to create an opening for a piercing attack.

"How did you...when? I destroyed it..."

"My Dark Knights are tough customers." Mira strolled up to the demon, each step a testament to her unshakable victory.

"How could I be defeated...like this?"

"I told you at the start—I'm a summoner."

"I...see."

Standing before Wolf Bane, Mira stared at him with her True Sight and Demon's Eye. He looked back, smiling faintly. His expression was one of respect at an honorable defeat.

The Dark Knight pulled its great sword free before readying the blade for another blow.

"Splendid..." Wolf Bane began to mutter an instant before the armor spirit chopped through the demon's neck. The body collapsed into a heap, and Wolf Bane's fallen head stared upward at the cave's ceiling in satisfaction.

Dark blood dripped from the spirit's blade, etching a black star into the bedrock that would never fade.

She Professed Herself Pupil of the Wise Man

"**U**NBELIEVABLE..." Asval muttered under his breath, having watched the entirety of the battle play out.

Emella and Zef were speechless. Flicker watched as the demon's magic dissipated.

Only Tact moved, sprinting across the rugged terrain with the Holy Knight in pursuit. Within moments, the members of Écarlate Carillon followed suit.

"Miss Mira, that was amazing! You're truly amazing!" the boy called as he approached.

"Hrmm, I suppose I am." Mira smirked as her eyes faded back to their normal state.

No vestige of her fight with the demon remained, and she was once again just a small girl whom most would underestimate. The tonal shift stunned the guild members for a moment before they too broke into smiles. All of them found their questions renewed as to who this girl was, and where she came from.

"I don't know what to say but thank you, Mira. You've saved us all," Emella said with a relieved smile.

"Yes, I don't know what we would have done if we'd been on our own."

"No thanks necessary. It was my fault you got caught up in all this."

"So Mira," Zephard interrupted, "is that why they jumped you all the way to C-Rank?"

Someone had to ask. It was a blunt question, but the situation called for nothing less.

"Hrmm, I suppose it won't hurt to tell you," she said, gesturing at the Holy Knight by Tact's side. Then she paused for dramatic effect.

"You mean the secret behind your strength?" asked Emella hoping to hurry her along.

"Have you heard of Danblf? I'm his pupil. He's...*indisposed* at the moment. So he's tasked me with handling some business on his behalf."

There it was, her cover story in a nutshell. Hopefully dropping the tidbit that she was related to the Nine Wise Men would allow her to handwave most other questions away if they got too pointed.

"Master Danblf's pupil, huh? No wonder you're so strong," Emella said, surprisingly unfazed by Mira's revelation.

"The One-Man Army...and you were trained by him." Asval nodded as if this was all perfectly reasonable.

And to an extent, it was.

The battle they witnessed had been of an untold magnitude, and the stone around them was pitted and scarred as a testament to the power that had been unleashed. Anyone who could wield such power clearly could not be constrained by the boundaries of common sense. Her previous erratic behavior became far more reasonable now that they knew she was in league with such extraordinary personages as the Nine Wise Men.

"Master Danblf... A pupil of the Wise Man..." Flicker stood repeating her answer over and over.

She had witnessed Mira's overwhelming power and had no doubt regarding her claim. In retrospect, this explained Mira's nonchalant attitude toward mana usage. But as a mage, she knew that this was an unprecedented situation for another reason.

It was an established fact that none of the Nine Wise Men had ever taken an apprentice. The scholars who labored in the Linked Silver Towers were just researchers—while they might often encounter the Wise Men, they would never share the strong bond of a true pupil-master relationship. None had ever been truly mentored by one of the Elders. This was a universal truth. Even Luminaria had never taken an apprentice in all the years since she'd returned.

Flicker found herself torn. On one hand, Mira's abilities could only be explained by her claim that she was Danblf's pupil. On the other hand, a pupil of a Wise Man was unheard of.

Meanwhile, Zef's hands flew in wild gestures as he gushed over the revelation. "Wow! *Of course* I know all about Danblf! That's incredible, Mira!" Turning his gaze to the Holy Knight standing beside her, he marveled, "This is something really special!"

Truth be told, he knew very little. Zef had never cared for the legendary tales that other kids loved, and he'd never been a student of history either. But regardless of who her teacher was, she'd toppled the demon, and that was good enough for Zephard. End of story.

To Tact—born long after the Wise Men had vanished—Mira was a greater hero than her master had ever been. He stared at her with stars in his eyes.

Mira's smirk faded to a nervous smile. She had expected more suspicion and questions to her claim and had been prepared to bluster her way through with bravado and calculated omissions of the truth. This was a bit anticlimactic, and she felt a little robbed.

With no challenges forthcoming, she calmed and sighed a small breath of relief, mumbling, "Hrmm, I didn't expect them to believe that so easily."

"Wait, it's not true?!" Emella's head snapped around as she overheard.

"What? No, it's true! Why are you so close?" Mira spat out as she blushed and backed away. "I...I just figured that since no one has seen my master in thirty years, you all would have had more to say on the subject."

"Good point." Emella nodded in agreement before reaching out to gently stroke the white knight.

Then, to Mira's chagrin, she began listing off rhetorical arguments against the claim.

"There are plenty of theories floating about regarding the whereabouts of the Wise Men. They've marched off into the

demon realm, they killed each other during a spectacular falling out, they attained godhood and ascended to heaven, and
so forth—but it's all speculation. Most believe that they've se-
questered themselves, hiding away from the mundane world and
refusing any further contact with mere mortals."

If she only knew how close to the truth she was, Mira thought as
she tried to keep her face composed.

Emella concluded, "But it's been thirty years since they vanished, so it's not that surprising that a pupil has appeared."

"And you know?" Asval broke in with a smile. "The way you
fight is just like the stories my father used to tell me."

"My father used to tell me those stories too!" chirped Tact.

"Me too," Flicker said. "Once it was discovered I had the latent
talents to be a mage, they told me stories of the Nine Wise Men
over and over again."

"Right?" Asval nodded. "I don't think there's anyone in this
country who hasn't heard all about those guys."

"Stories? What stories?" Mira muttered as her eyebrows
arched suspiciously. Hopefully, they were flattering.

"You haven't heard the legend of King Solomon and the Nine
Wise Men?!" Emella shouted in surprise, the loudest she'd been
all day. When Mira nodded, she smiled and said, "Well, that
won't do."

She launched into the tales. The stories were very popular
throughout the Kingdom of Alcait regardless of gender or age,
and nearly everyone knew them by heart. One of the stories,
called The One-Man Army, focused on Danblf and told the tale

of him summoning a thousand armor spirits in a single battle. But the most popular story about the Elder summoner told of when he'd been forced into close combat and how he had used both his summoning wizardry and immortal arts to carry the day.

Emella retold the tale with stars in her eyes—how his summons had flown through the air as Danblf controlled the ground.

Since the group had grown up with such stories, it was no wonder they immediately accepted Mira's claims.

"I had no idea," Mira muttered to herself while Tact sat next to her, enchanted by the story even though he had heard it hundreds of times before.

"And that's just the beginning, Mira! Your master's bravery doesn't end there!" Emella pumped her fist in the air and got ready to tell another, when Flicker's staff bopped her on the side of her head.

"That's enough for the moment. I think it's time to head back. There's a lot to report."

"R-right. Led's do dat..." Emella said as she staggered back to her feet with tears in her eyes.

"Eh, that was probably my fault," Mira said gently. "I suppose I should have stopped you at some point."

"Don't worry about it, Mira," Flicker said with a wicked, satisfied grin as she approached her. "Emella was the one at fault!"

With panther-like reflexes, she scooped Mira into her arms. Shoving her face into Mira's chest, Flicker began breathing heavily and rubbing her with her cheeks. For a mage, the strike was unbelievably agile and precise.

"What?!" howled Mira. "Put me down!"

A chilly breeze blew across the pair in the wake of a well-placed karate chop, and the beast dropped its prey. Flicker lay on the ground, clutching her shoulder, as Emella stood ready to deliver another blow.

It seemed the pair were well versed in halting each other's outbursts.

"Sorry about that," Emella said.

"She'd been keeping it together so well," murmured Mira.

"I think as the adrenaline rush faded, the self-control went with it."

"Seems like a chore to manage."

They watched Flicker writhe on the ground, a smile on her face, whispering to herself, "Worth it. She was so soft!"

"Just part of who she is," Asval grunted with a sigh.

"So Mira, you can use both summoning magic and immortal arts together just like Master Danblf?" said Emella. "That's amazing."

"Immortal arts, huh?" mused Zef, looking thoughtfully at his daggers. "Was that how you vanished? It was incredible."

"That's a pretty standard technique, actually," Mira said flatly.

"It was too fast for me to follow at some points. Are you saying all Sages can move like that?"

"All pretty standard."

"Didn't you even run on air at one point? We've got a Sage in our guild, but I don't think they can do that."

"A skill called Air Step. Also pretty standard."

The grandeur of the battle that they'd seen would be etched in their minds forever. She was happy to see that the opinion of the immortal arts had greatly risen among the members of Écarlate Carillon.

Then again, she was the pupil of one of the Wise Men who wielded the immortal arts and triumphed in a fated battle. A fated battle in which she overcame a demon. How could they not be mesmerized by what they'd seen?

Mira smirked, and then her eyes widened in shock.

"Wait...what?"

She'd been hoping to show off her summoning skills! Now it appeared that her Sage combat skills were getting all the accolades. She stared off into the distance and wondered where it had all gone wrong.

"I want to be an amazing mage just like you, Miss Mira!" Tact beamed at her, taking some of the bite out of her realization.

"Oho, do you, now? You want to be a *summoner* like me, do you? A fine decision!" Mira smiled happily as she patted him on the head.

"If you want to be a mage, first thing to do is check to see if you have the aptitude," Flicker said. "I wonder if you'll have the spark?"

"The aptitude?" Mira looked puzzled.

"Ah, you haven't heard?"

"Hrmm, no. My master took me far from civilization for my training." Mira amended her cover on the fly. "I'm not familiar with it."

"I see…" Flicker said slowly, narrowing her eyes. "I suppose I can explain. Simply put, everyone has some level of magical power—some small, some large. That difference determines the level of spells they can cast, and it's measured as a score of their magical aptitude. Only those with a sufficient magical aptitude are trained to become mages, since a low score would make the profession a poor career choice."

Back in *Ark Earth Online*, players had the freedom to excel at any class they wanted, provided they put in the effort—anyone could be anything. But now, it seemed people no longer had that freedom of choice. Magical power was determined at birth.

"Magical aptitude, eh? Well, what about Tact here? Can he become a summoner?"

"There's no way to tell until we check. They do examinations at the Mages' Guild, so you could probably get one done when we get back to town."

"Isn't that convenient? Well, Tact, what do you think? Want to find out?"

"You'd do that for me, Miss Mira? Of course I want to know!"

"Well, then, let's stop by when we get back." Mira cast Tact a soft smile.

Flicker's smile was much more rueful, wishing she were the object of Mira's attention.

She Professed Herself Pupil of the Wise Man

14

"**H**EY! You think we might get anything good from this?"

Mira was still imagining the impending wave of new summoners when Zef's voice rang out. Looking over, she saw him rolling the demon's corpse over with the toe of his boot to free the war scythe from where it lay on the ground.

"It's even crazier up close." Asval stooped down to look at the demon's body, inspecting all the various wounds and scars. Tapping it with his knuckles, he sighed at the strange resilience of the monster's hide, wondering if he would have even stood a chance against it.

He glanced at Emella, and her hand reflexively drifted to the pommel of her sword as the same doubt raced through her mind. She decided to double her training from that point onward. As images from the battle lingered, she couldn't quell the worry that this would not be the last time she would encounter such a foe.

While the adventurers got a closer look at the corpse, Tact hid himself behind Mira. She gently squeezed his hand and offered reassurance. "Don't worry. It can't hurt you now."

Flicker loitered behind, watching the scene and calculating the best moment to snatch Mira's other free hand.

"So...problem," said Zef, stooping down to grab the scythe. "I don't think I can carry this."

Reaching down to assist, Asval immediately regretted his decision. "Oof! How can it be that heavy?"

Using both hands, he managed to get it in the air for a moment before it came crashing back down. The blade shrieked as the tip buried itself in the stone.

"So what do you think?" asked Zephard.

"It has to be some class-specific item. I'm a warrior and I can't use it—and I doubt the little miss needs a weapon. She'll probably get a pretty coin when she sells it."

"Right? Between this and all the Mobility Stones, Mira's made out like a bandit. You think she'll give me a cut for being her loot caddy?" Zef smiled jokingly.

"What kind of nonsense are you talking about?" Mira's sudden response wiped Zephard's smile off his face. Then she continued. "Naturally, we'll all get equal shares. Numbers aren't my forte, so someone else, figure out what the split is."

The members of Écarlate Carillon stared at her in shock. Between the Mobility Stones and the scythe—an actual demon's weapon—this raid would be worth a small fortune. By all rights, the lion's share belonged to Mira, since she had carried the party—but her turn of generosity had granted them a sizable boon.

"Are you sure about that, Mira?" Emella asked hesitantly.

"We're a party, aren't we?"

Both she and Emella stood and looked at the other in confusion. That was the opportunity Flicker needed to strike.

"You're so wonderful, Mira!" the purple-robed mage cooed as she lunged forward and pulled Mira into a hug.

The summoner visually pleaded with Emella for assistance, and soon a rain of chops fell upon Flicker's head.

"You're just full of surprises, Mira," Asval said with a grateful nod.

"I'd have to agree," said Emella with a bemused smile.

"I'm just not all that concerned with matters of money." Mira waved her hand as if to say that the treasure was nothing—but in the back of her mind, she knew that if her own funds dried up, she could always mooch off of Solomon.

"Considering the hotel you're staying in, that makes sense," said Emella with a distant look in her eyes. She toyed with the idea of splurging on a few nights of luxury after she cashed out.

"Oh, that's right," muttered Asval.

"You did tell us about that," said Zef. He and Asval recalled the glittering décor and the lavish feast. "It'd be nice not to have to worry about money."

"Well, there you go. Like I said, money isn't an issue."

"Are you absolutely certain?"

"Drop it. And if there's anyone in your guild who you think might make use of the scythe, it's theirs. Better that it goes to someone who will get some use out of it." Whenever equipment was found in the game, it went to the party member who could make the most use of it. It was how things had been done in her day, and she saw no reason to change it.

Flicker, who had just come to, looked on in confusion. "We'll have to get it appraised, but this alone..."

"I insist. It'll always be worth more to a friend than the money I would have gotten for it. I don't want it—would any of your guildmates?"

"Hmmm. We do have a dark knight in the guild. He might be able to wield it." Asval said.

"Oho, a dark knight? Well, there you go. Give it to him."

"No, but... Mira, we're grateful for anything that helps out the guild," Emella protested with a blush of embarrassment. "But we can't accept this. We just can't."

"She's right." Asval nodded. "We appreciate the offer, but I'm just not comfortable with taking it like that."

But Mira didn't need the scythe or the money, and she shook her head as she refused to be swayed.

"Look. I know I can trust the Écarlate Carillon. I'd rather see it stay with allies then swap it for cash and face it in the hands of an enemy on some other battlefield."

She may not have known them for long, but she had no lingering doubts as to the guild's character. The fact that they'd tagged along just to ensure Tact's welfare told her enough.

Her gaze shifted from the scythe back to Emella. As their eyes met, Emella looked stunned, but gradually her expression brightened. Mira offered her hand.

"All right, then! We'll take care of it!" Emella shook the summoner's hand.

With a grumble and a roll of his eyes, Asval bent down to

pick up the weapon. Zephard grinned and bent over to pick up the other end.

"Seems a little hasty to me," grumbled the big warrior as he and the rogue hauled the weapon over to the vice captain.

"If anything happens, I'll just come back personally to retrieve it—how about that?" Mira asked wryly.

"Fair."

"Well, then, as it's now our responsibility, I'll take care of it." Emella opened her Item Box and loaded the scythe inside. Visible only to her, the capacity counter increased dangerously toward her User's Bangle's max load. "Oof. Close fit. Maybe with the cash from this raid, I can upgrade my storage limit."

"I can take some of your excess equipment if you need to make room," Asval offered.

Mira tilted her head in confusion, then stepped a little closer to get a better look at Emella's bangle. "Hrmm... You have limits on your carrying capacity?"

"You don't?" Emella responded, equally puzzled.

Zef stood with a stunned look on his face. As the designated looter, he was often forced to make hard choices about what to keep and what to leave behind on their adventures.

With a sudden concern that she'd missed an incredibly important difference between the game and the new world, Mira opened her own Item Box to check her inventory. She didn't seem to be carrying any single thing that was particularly heavy, but she was carrying small stuff...*lots* of small stuff. The sum total of her odds and ends weighed close to half a ton.

There wasn't any indicated maximum capacity, but if there was, then she was confident that it was quite high.

"Hrmm... I'm carrying a fair bit, but I wonder—"

"The guild must have said something about the capacity," Flicker interjected.

"Yeah," said Emella. "That's always part of the rental agreement."

That reminded Mira that none of the Écarlate Carillon had been with her at the Mages' Guild. In a moment of panic, she wondered if she had just blown her cover by asking about something as mundane as inventory management systems.

"Ah...you see," she said haltingly, "this was entrusted to me by my master. All he taught me was how to use it."

Emella nodded slowly. "Ah, well, I suppose that would explain it."

In her head, Mira ran through other follow-up questions the party might ask, trying to hedge against spilling any more of the truth. She decided that to simply profess ignorance would be the best path—her master had kept her away from the world, thus she only knew what Danblf knew.

Flicker narrowed her eyes. "Even so, running out of carry capacity could be a nasty surprise when you least expect it. You may want to get that checked at some point."

"That's very true," Mira said with a vigorous nod of her head. "Wise counsel. I'll have to make sure to do so."

Certainly not with the Mages' Guild, though. Mira made a mental note to take the issue up with Solomon next time they were behind closed doors. But the specter of doubt still loomed over her.

"Say, would you all mind helping me run a field test...just to be sure?" she asked.

The rest of the party looked at one another and shrugged before agreeing.

First, they transferred the scythe into Mira's Item Box. Though it took the help of Asval and Zephard to move the weapon once it was out of Emella's inventory, the scythe went neatly into Mira's Item Box and left her feeling no heavier. Next were multiple pieces of heavy equipment from Asval's inventory, and even the massive war hammer he carried.

The rest of the party seemed very impressed as she returned the stock, hoping that her curiosity hadn't given any of them further clues about her true nature.

As the experiment wrapped up, Zef called out in shock, "Whoa! It's burning!"

The rest of the party spun and saw the corpse of the demon engulfed in black flame.

"What happened? What'd you do?!" Asval asked as he approached where Zef stood near the edge of the flame.

"Me?! I didn't do anything! I was just looking at it, then this happened." Zef shook his head, the flickering fire reflected in his eyes.

"Don't worry about it. That's just what demons do a few minutes after death," Mira said, looking slightly bored before amending, "At least, that's what Master Danblf told me."

"Th-there're some things left in the fire," muttered Zef, cautiously poking at a black object with one of his daggers.

Once they had cooled, he carefully placed the items into his inventory.

With their final tasks completed, the party ascended from the bottom floor of the dungeon. None of the monsters had yet returned, so the journey was long and uneventful. Finally passing through the ward at the top of Ancient Temple Nebrapolis, they all took a moment to savor a few breaths of fresh air.

"Phew. This moment always feels so good." Emella exhaled deeply and stretched—even the oppressive atmosphere in the ritual hall was a relief, compared to the dank, gloomy levels below the surface.

Asval and Flicker took a moment to relax, while Zef muttered in pain and held a hand gingerly over his cheek. A red handprint was still visible from where he'd taken his teasing of Emella a step too far on the lowest set of stairs. Tact scanned the party members, committing the moment to memory and resolving to become an adventurer himself.

Crimson rays spilled in through the cracks of the partially collapsed temple entrance.

"Well, we finished that earlier than I'd expected," Emella said cheerfully, before her expression clouded. "We might be able to make it back to the city before the sun goes down."

It took just under an hour to walk back from the Ancient Temple Nebrapolis to Karanak—but Emella had planned for a quest that would take at least two days and one night, with the party having to camp in one of the middle levels of the dungeon. Her Item Box was still packed full of food and camping gear that was no longer needed. To make matters worse, all of it was in disarray after being displaced by the bulk of the scythe.

"All the way to the bottom of the Ancient Temple and back in under a day," Asval mused, turning to look back at the temple. The statues on the cliff wall cast dark shadows in the waning light of day, their expressions more ominous at dusk. "This'll make for an interesting yarn to tell at the pub."

"Encountering a demon is definitely exciting material," Zef said with a grin.

Flicker's expression darkened as she cast the rogue a dubious look. "I don't think exciting is the right word for it."

"Fair enough."

The demons had been banished ten years ago. News of their reemergence would surely cause panic.

"Maybe we should keep this to ourselves." Emella pursed her lips and placed her hand on the hilt of her spirit blade. "We'll tell the captain before we make any big decisions. In any case, let's get the heck out of here."

The party voiced their agreement, including Zef, who was notoriously loose-lipped around the ladies. He looked crestfallen as he realized he couldn't impress any girls with stories of his adventures this evening. Then he stopped and looked back at the Ancient Temple.

With a sigh and a tear in his eye, he wished he could go back to the fifth level just one more time.

She Professed Herself Herself Pupil of the Wise Man

15

AN HOUR AFTER they'd set off, the dense forest surrounding the road gave way and they saw the gates of Karanak before them. The sun melted into the horizon on the hills above the city, staining the buildings a deep scarlet as the brightest stars began to twinkle in the heavens.

The city should have begun to show the excitement of night-life, but the scene that spread before them was excitement of a completely different sort.

"What in the world?" Emella gasped as her hand reached for her sword.

Packs of beasts rampaged through the city, squaring off against adventurers and the Knight Patrol alike.

"Come on! We have to help!" Asval shouted as he ran toward the sound of fighting, Emella and Zef close on his heels.

"Tact, should we go find your grandfather?" Mira asked as she tightened her grip on the boy's hand.

"He'll be fine. Grandpa's the strongest guy in the city!" he said pridefully.

"All right. Stay close and don't get separated from me."

"Okay!"

Deciding that a little extra insurance was never a bad policy, Mira summoned her Holy Knight and ordered the spirit to guard Tact.

"I've got your back," Flicker said, moving closer to the pair.

With Emella gone, who would keep a firm hand on her leash? Mira hustled to catch up to the other three party members with Tact in tow.

"Are these the same zombies?" Mira muttered as she passed by monsters cut down by the trio. They were certainly made of vegetation and compost like the others, yet something was different.

"These aren't humanoid like the ones before. Where did they come from?!" Emella said, gracefully reaching out to snatch Flicker away from Mira as she and Tact caught up to the rest of the group.

It was undeniable. Previously, the zombies had looked more or less human in form, but these were undeniably beast-shaped. Their sudden turn toward aggression was also a new development.

The beast-type zombies were overrunning Karanak. Cries and sounds of battle came from every direction while the streetlights silently illuminated the carnage of the city below. The human casualties were blessedly minor compared to the damage wrought on the city itself—so far. It seemed that the guild had efficiently mobilized and was prioritizing protecting lives over property.

"Hrmm... What the...?" Mira mumbled to herself, looking at the ruined front of an umbrella shop. A dead humanoid zombie lay propped up against the broken storefront with an open parasol clutched in its hand. It looked like it had died trying to keep out of a sudden rainstorm.

She chuckled at the absurd sight, then stopped and eyed the scene suspiciously.

"Let's make our way to the central plaza." Emella pointed down the street toward an intersection packed with zombies being driven back by adventurers. "We'll pass the guild offices and a patrol station along the way. Maybe they'll know something."

"Hrmm, indeed." Mira nodded, but then she paused as something familiar caught her eye. "Hey, I know that carriage..."

She squinted as she tried to make it out through the dim evening light, then ran forward so she could get a better look.

Zombies swarmed in from the alleyways and shadows to intercept, but they were cut to pieces by a Dark Knight before they could reach her. The form in dark armor fell in with Emella and the others as they struggled to keep pace with the diminutive summoner.

The carriage lay on its side, where it had plowed into one of the buildings lining the main street. Two horses pawed impatiently at the cobblestones, still tethered to the driver's post by their reins. Sure enough, it was the same carriage that carried Mira to the city a few days earlier—and a body wearing a familiar military uniform was sprawled on the sidewalk nearby.

"Garrett! Hold on." Mira bent down to roll him over and give him a shake. As she did, he groaned and a grin crept across his face.

She pulled back with a start. Looking around the area, zombie corpses littered the street and sidewalk, and the sides of the broken carriage were covered in muddy red stains. She'd seen that color before.

"Come on, Garrett, get up!" Mira smacked at Garrett's smiling cheeks as he began to giggle uncontrollably.

"Ugh... Ah, an angel! Which means this must be heaven?"

"It's me, you fool of a vice commander! What have you done?" Mira kneaded her forehead in despair as she gestured to the carriage beside them.

"Ah, ohhh. About that..." he mumbled as the rest of the party caught and looked around with a mixture of awe and shock. As he regained his senses, he told the story.

Around midday, the usual human zombies had appeared and had begun to roam the streets. While distressing to the city, the strange event was peaceful—at first. Not long after, zombie beasts appeared. Looking like bears, wolves, and other ferocious creatures, these zombies began to attack the residents of the town.

The Knight Patrol was rapidly overwhelmed by reports across the city and activated emergency plans. The Fighters' Guild was converted into a shelter to house panicked townsfolk, and the Mages' Guild was rapidly transformed into a field hospital. Adventurers from both the main guilds and private guilds began to retake the town as the Knight Patrol coordinated their efforts. They went from house to house, checking in on townsfolk who were safely sheltering behind locked doors.

Garrett had been at the guild offices on business when the call to action was issued. His carriage was just outside and, well... while his defensive driving skills left much to be desired, his *offensive* driving skills were not found wanting.

"Just part of my military duty," he said emphatically.

"I've never seen anything like this," Mira remarked. Looking down the street, the zombie corpses were littered across the city. The efforts of adventurers continued to add to the number of fallen beasts.

"This is going to be a mess to clean up," Mira said glumly.

"A backbreaking task, to be sure," added Zef.

A moment of silence followed as the assembled group heaved a collective sigh of despair for tomorrow's chores.

"It would be easier with the FAV," Garrett said after the pause, walking around the fallen carriage to inspect for damage.

"Hrmm... That seems like overkill." Mira wondered if the zombies or Garrett would have done more damage if the Fast Armored Vehicle had been in play. "The carriage seems to be fine... besides lying sideways."

"They build them with VIP transport in mind. They're tougher than they look." Garrett stroked the side of the vehicle lovingly.

"I see..." said Mira, recognizing the signs of obsession and retreating a few steps.

After Garrett's tender moment had passed, Asval, Emella, and Zef helped him right the vehicle with a count of three and a mighty heave-ho. The carriage creaked as it settled back onto its suspension. It was none worse for the wear besides the filthy, zombie-stained sides.

"Can I give you guys a lift?"

"We're fine," Mira responded before anyone could take Garrett up on his offer.

"Pity."

"Hrmm."

After an awkward pause, Garrett climbed back onto the driver's seat. "Well, duty calls."

"I'm sure it does."

"Take care, Mira. I'll see you when this is over."

With that, he cracked the reins and plunged back into battle with a cry on his lips. Protected by their technomancy harnesses, the horses sprinted forward with brave whinnies, trampling the zombies before them.

Mira watched him ride off with a blank look on her face.

"Do you know him, Mira?" asked Emella, "He was a royal soldier, wasn't he?"

"He's a menace."

Thanks to Garrett's situation report, the party no longer had to divert to the guild offices for instruction. They proceeded to the town square, sweeping away all foes as they advanced.

Emella and Asval slashed and smashed zombies to the front while Zef and Flicker took care of any stragglers on the flanks.

Ahead, Mira's Dark Knight raged relentlessly, amassing quite the body count.

And yet still the zombies kept coming.

"There's no end to this," grumbled Mira.

Unaccustomed to the considerations that had to be made while wearing a skirt—and unaware of the twinkle in Flicker's eye below—Mira kicked away a lunging beast as she nimbly scrambled to the top of a building and looked around at the surrounding city.

While individually weak, the zombies were appearing in waves, and their sheer volume threatened to wear down the defenders. From her perch, she could see pockets of skilled warriors scattered across the city, and they all looked to be withdrawing to more defensible positions.

Maybe...this is an opportunity! she mused. A perfect chance to show off the power of summoning.

Spreading both arms wide, she initiated Bound Arcana and immediately shifted into the Mark of the Rosary. She began to chant.

A silent wake under the moonlight—the grave marker an unsheathed sword.

The myriad colors from the heavens guide your way.

Ripped from the eternal wheel, the maidens called to battle.

Their swords play a dirge and cut a rainbow through the skies.

Descend to me from the evening sky, my chosen seven clad in light!

[Evocation: Valkyrie Sisters]

Every word melted into the night, dyeing the magic circles with the colors of the rainbow. As the last word was spoken and spun into a single desire, the circles brilliantly shone with Mira's power and Alfina descended—but this time, she was not alone.

Her sisters followed behind, passing through the rings and appearing one after another. The magic circles collapsed into a bead of light and dispersed as the last appeared.

"The Sisters Seven answer your summons." Alfina stepped forward with the other six behind her.

Standing on the rooftop, they knelt as one in honor of Mira. Each was clad in similar but slightly different armor; all were beautiful and noble beyond compare.

"Hrmm, indeed. Hi again, Alfina. It's been a while since I've seen the rest of you. Are you doing well?" Mira asked. She'd known them only as summoned NPCs and was curious to see how they'd react.

"Fine, apart from Alfina's training regime!" responded one, almost as if tattling on her older sister. She quickly dropped her gaze to escape Alfina's pointed glare.

Alfina bowed deeply. "Apologies for that, my lady. Christina shall receive a stern talking to later."

Christina was the youngest of the Valkyrie sisters, with her hair done up in pigtails and her armor bearing the mark of a heart. Alfina was the eldest, and the two were nearly polar opposites.

"Hrmm, she's been keeping the training tough, has she?"

"It is an easy training method that emphasizes repetition of the basic fundamentals..." Alfina began.

Christina quickly interrupted. "A hundred thousand repetitions is easy?!"

Mira was inclined to agree. "I see. A hundred thousand does seem like quite a bit."

Perhaps they had been interrupted mid-training session or just finished with one when she summoned them. Upon closer inspection, the sisters seemed exhausted. Mira looked at the group with a mixture of pity and pride.

"We must continue to train so that we may be of use to you, Master!" Alfina said with an uncompromising gaze.

"Hrmm, is that so?" She was about to let the issue slide when she saw the rest of the sisters behind Alfina pleading to her with desperate eyes. "Were you all just training a moment ago?"

"Of course. We practice whenever we're not sleeping or eating."

Her sisters grimaced and hung their heads.

"Just so." Mira contemplated how to answer. "Alfina...perhaps some rest periods are in order. I have returned and might call upon you at any time. It wouldn't do to have you tired and battered from training."

"But I..." Alfina's eyes widened and she turned to look at her sisters, all of whom looked exhausted. Then she bowed low. "Master, please forgive me! I was focused on being prepared for your summons and have committed a grievous mistake."

"No apology necessary for an error of good intent," said Mira, placing a hand on Alfina's shoulder. "Rather, thank you for your efforts. But from here on out, maintain battle readiness."

"Your words are too kind. I shall review our training regime as you suggest."

Hopefully, that settles things, Mira thought as she backed up and glanced at the relieved expressions of the sisters.

"Wonderful. Now to the matter at hand. The city has a zombie infestation, and I need you all to take care of it. How about it? Are you up to the task?"

"Yes! Leave it to us!" Christina answered immediately.

Now she wore a lively smile and seemed to brim with energy. The rest of the sisters seemed equally resolute.

"Hrmm. Very encouraging." Mira nodded in satisfaction at their response before handing over the reins. "Well, then, Alfina, I'll leave you in charge. The faster we wrap this up, the better."

"It shall be done."

After another deep bow, Alfina stood and lifted her sword to the heavens. Her sisters rose to their feet and unsheathed their weapons with pride before doing the same.

"We are the Sisters Seven! As our lady wills it!" Their voices were adamant and their eyes burned with devotion.

"To battle! Advance!" Alfina shouted. Her sisters vanished in a sudden blur of motion, and with a final bow, she sprang onto the battlefield herself.

After watching them go, Mira jumped off the roof to rejoin the party, much to Flicker's delight.

16

THE VALKYRIES were not subtle. Within moments of taking their place on the field of battle, they dazzled the citizens with their martial prowess and unmatched beauty. Valiant adventurers on the verge of being overwhelmed suddenly found themselves reinforced. Their morale soared as the tide of the fight turned against the undead.

As the number of zombies diminished, the defenders began to go on the hunt in active search for the dwindling number of beasts. Often, they would find themselves beaten to the task by another group of adventurers or one of the Valkyrie sisters.

"No matter how many zombies there are, they're just a rabble with the Valkyries here," Asval observed during a brief pause. "Guess this is what I can expect from the pupil of the One-Man Army."

Shouldering his large hammer, Asval glanced about with a relaxed smile. All around him, the zombies had been halted as they were cut down by adventurers. Whether trapped in narrow alleys and dispensed with spears and polearms, hacked apart with axes and swords, or bludgeoned with maces and quarterstaffs, none of the beasts seemed up to the challenge of taking on the combined might of the guild members and the Valkyrie sisters. It was only a matter of time until the city was secure.

Or so he believed.

"Master! Look to the sky!" Alfina landed in their midst and glared upward.

Something was floating above them. Surrounded by a black mist, the stars obscured by the object seemed diminished, as though they had been infected by a slow-acting poison.

"What is that?" Mira frowned as she looked up and tried to make out the hovering figure in the darkness.

"The nature of its magic leads me to believe it's a half-demon," Alfina replied.

"A half-demon?!" Mira could hardly believe it.

Abominations born of the union between a demon and a human, they were beings of solitude. Unable to become true demons due to their human ancestry, and unwelcome among humanity because of their corrupted power.

"Yes, but..." Alfina seemed to be at a loss for words for a moment. "My lady, I believe this one...this one is *dead*."

"Oho, another zombie, then?"

"Y-yes. It seems that a strange magical power blanketing the area is the cause of both. The cause is yet unknown, but it's indiscriminately reanimating buried corpses and causing them to run amok. I have procured a sample for you to review."

Each of the Valkyrie sisters possessed a special set of skills, and Alfina bore a sphere that could condense and contain magical energy. As she spoke, she produced a small globe and held it before Mira. The orb was so black, it appeared as a hole in space resting atop her palm, and Mira peered at it with curiosity.

"Hrmm, so that's what we're dealing with, eh?" Mira arched an eyebrow. The effect of an orb would vary depending on the quantity and type of magic it contained, but this one was surely dangerous.

"This could be put to use, should you desire. What is your opinion, Master?" Alfina asked.

It was tempting. There would be battles to come, and the ability to reanimate the fallen and send them back into the fight might come in handy. Mira pondered for a moment, then sighed and said, "We don't need it. Get rid of it."

"Understood." Looking slightly relieved, Alfina banished the orb. "What shall we do about the half-demon?"

"If the zombies were created from nearby corpses, then that half-demon must have been buried somewhere in the vicinity," Mira surmised, peering into the sky.

"I would agree."

Mira wondered what that meant. Half-demons were a rare species and very conspicuous. Why would one have been buried in a place like this? From the fog of memory, she recalled something from the past.

There had once been buzz among players about a strange and hostile NPC. It appeared out of nowhere, was overwhelmingly strong, and would attack players on sight. After a number of players had been killed, there was an official announcement made regarding a sudden in-game event. The goal was to eliminate a half-demon that was running rampant across the continent.

Thousands participated. Thousands were killed.

Despite numerous respawns, the players finally succeeded in bringing down their foe somewhere near Karanak, City of Requiem. Mira—well, Danblf—had been present at the final moment, of course. As such, Mira was well acquainted with the power and abilities of a half-demon.

"This is going to be quite a nuisance," she grumbled while squinting skyward.

"I'm sure you can handle such a foe, my lady."

"Indeed. The first time we met, I was quite a bit less experienced. It was a difficult encounter." Mira gave a wry smirk.

"Was the fight truly that difficult? Then we should strike before it completely revives itself."

"What's that? You're saying it's not yet completely revived?"

"Correct. My sisters and I have this in hand, my lady. No need to concern yourself with this foul beast."

Mira felt relieved and disappointed at the same time. With a hint of haughtiness in her voice, she replied, "Hrmm, very well. Show me what you can do."

"It would be my pleasure," Alfina said with a bow before rising with a cold smile. "I have but one request, Master. Will you authorize Imitation Code G?"

"That's a new one. Going to try a new technique on this thing?"

"You are correct, Master," Alfina said with the same cool smile.

It was common practice for players to take opportunities for test runs of new skills, spells, or techniques to make sure that they were comfortable with their usage. That a former NPC was about to do the same was a sign of how much the world had changed. Alfina's elated anticipation of trying a new technique on a worthy foe was a feeling Mira could both understand and relate to.

"Then by all means." Mira nodded and gestured at the floating form in the sky.

"With your blessing, my lady." Alfina bowed and leapt away, running down the main street as if gliding through the air.

Danblf would often invite observers when he attempted a new summoning. Now, the Valkyrie sisters—her summons!—were about to wow Mira and the assembled adventurers battling the incursion all across the city.

She might not know much about necromancy, but there was no doubt that the discipline of summoning was about to come screaming back from the grave. Mira chuckled to herself at the thought.

Unwilling to miss the coming show, Mira scrambled up to the roof of a nearby building that offered a good view of what was to come.

A moment later, Alfina appeared with her sisters arrayed in formation around her. They jumped, each landing on a different rooftop and raising their weapons to the sky. Rays of light stretched from their swords to converge below the black mist, drawing a circle of light in the heavens.

"This is certainly something, isn't it?" said Mira to herself, wishing she had some popcorn.

The luminous magic circle enlarged, and elaborate crests began to appear around its rim. As it glimmered and gleamed, the fighting on the ground came to a halt as all eyes were drawn upward.

Seven pillars of light soared skyward, and Alfina leapt to land in the middle of the hovering magic circle.

Those designs resemble a summoning circle, Mira thought as she looked at Alfina and waited for what might happen next.

With the whole city watching, Alfina bent down and plunged her hand into the magic circle. The light converged and swelled before bursting an instant later in a brilliant flash.

As onlookers blinked to banish the afterimage, Alfina descended. In her right hand, she bore a golden spear, and her eyes were fixed on the half-demon hovering above.

"Die!" she bellowed, launching the golden spear skyward. In the blink of an eye, it was a ray of light that pierced her foe and continued up into the stars.

First came the roar—rising like distant thunder. Then a shockwave swept across Karanak, shattering windows and blowing light objects into the street. Then came the light, a growing luminosity that shone like the sun.

In the dark of night, Karanak was lit up as though it were midday. Anyone on the ground who was foolish enough to stare into the light found themselves unable to see for a few minutes after it had faded.

"The half-demon is defeated, and the magic energy erased," Alfina reported, dropping onto the rooftop next to Mira.

"Hrmm, very well done." Mira blinked away the afterimage of the blast as the rest of the sisters joined their eldest sibling. "A splendid technique."

"We are honored by your praise, my lady." Alfina bowed, allowing a smile to leak onto her normally stoic face. The other six were less reserved and let their pride shine as they bowed as well.

"Well, good job. Go get some rest." Finally able to see the sisters again, Mira prepared to send them back.

"As you command," replied Alfina as light began to envelop her.

Christina in particular looked overjoyed. She grinned and gave a thumbs-up as she faded away.

Mira looked back over the city, now much quieter. She shimmied her way back off the rooftop and found the rest of her party.

"Mira, did I just see Alfina throwing a spear? What was that?!" Emella babbled as she approached.

"They said it was a new technique."

"A new technique?" Asval arched an eyebrow and let out a low whistle. "That was some power."

"Shoot, did the sisters already leave?" asked Zef, disappointed.

Mira took a moment to appreciate that the rogue had his priorities and he stuck by them.

"A new spear-throwing technique?" Emella muttered to herself, resolving to bring the matter up with Alfina should she ever encounter the Valkyrie again.

"Whatever it was, it looks like it got the job done. That summoning of yours is quite a power." Asval smiled in admiration.

Mira's smirk was astronomical in scale. "Exactly! Exactly as I said! Tell your friends. Tell everyone."

Through all of this, Flicker just kept looking up into the sky. She appeared to be in ecstasy, as if she had seen a truly revelatory sight.

After a few more hours on alert, the Knight Patrol and the guilds jointly declared an end to the emergency. Citizens sheltering in the guild buildings were allowed to leave and return to their homes, while knights and guild members looked on in envy. It was time for cleanup.

The time was nearing seven in the evening, and many people tried to resume normal life as swiftly as possible. Some shops reopened, and many pubs tried to attract patrons.

Mira, Tact, Emella, and Flicker mingled with the onlookers in the center of the street, while Asval and Zef helped stack the remains of some zombies onto a wagon to be disposed of.

"Is the whole city like this?" Emella muttered while watching. "It'll take days to clear this all away."

"Leave it long enough and I'm sure we'll have new forms of undead on our hands," Flicker said, staring at the pile.

"Ugh! Don't say that!" Emella pursed her lips and tried to imagine what might emerge.

As if summoned by that thought, something nearby suddenly began to stir. A moment later, Mira saw a form emerge.

"Hey! Something's still moving!" called an onlooker as a humanoid figure crawled out of the pile so slowly that everyone stopped to watch instead of springing to action.

Eventually, the zombie slowly stood up. Its vacant face, made of dirt and vegetation, scanned the crowd as though searching for something.

Then someone in the crowd let out a bone-chilling scream.

The zombie stopped moving and stared. Its gaze was fixed on a plump woman of middle age standing near Mira. The onlookers started to murmur as they watched the scene unfold.

Unsettled by the ominous stare, the woman stepped back to escape the gaze of the zombie and it tried to give chase—but the creature's body had reached its limit. It lurched forward and stumbled, then crawled, dragging its feet behind it like withered stalks. The terrified woman screamed again and slumped to the ground in fright.

Mira and Emella moved closer to the woman and took a defensive stance, keeping themselves in a blocking position, and a moment later, a Knight Patrol officer stepped forward. His sword flashed through the air, leaving a shining trail in the light of the streetlamp.

Cut in two, the pitiful wretch crumbled silently to the ground and stirred no further. There was a brief moment of silence, then a burst of applause as the people commended the officer for his quick response.

"Hrmm... Was that zombie trying to say something?" Mira placed her finger to her chin.

At the moment of its collapse, Mira thought she saw its mouth trying to form a word. But whatever it said was too quiet for her to hear. Perhaps it hadn't said anything at all.

"Mother." Emella stared at the corpse.

"Hrmm?"

"It said, '*Mother.*'"

As Mira turned about, she saw the stunned look on Emella's face. Apparently, she had heard the zombie's last word but could scarcely believe that the creature had managed to say anything at all.

"I wonder what it meant?" Mira thought back to the incident.

The zombie's face had been as expressionless as a broken clay figure—yet somehow, it seemed melancholy, as if it bore a great weight. She stepped closer to the corpse to inspect the pitiful creature.

There was something in the gap between the tattered cloak and scarred leather armor. Reaching down to pluck the item from the corpse, she found it was long and thin and wrapped in luxurious cloth. Inside was a scuffed dagger.

"Isn't that a memento blade?" Emella asked, peaking over Mira's shoulder at the blade in her hands.

"Is that so?"

"I think it is. The scabbard is engraved with the symbols of the trinity, after all."

Sure enough, carved in the wooden scabbard—somewhat awkwardly—were the symbols.

"It's a bit rough, but you're absolutely right. Any other observations?" Mira asked, hoping to learn more of the dagger, and more of the world that had existed during her thirty-year absence. She remembered the temples dedicated to the three gods, but she passed the blade to Emella to find out what other information the elven swordswoman might have.

An instant later, the plump woman had snatched it from Emella's grasp. "Please, let me see that!"

While she and Mira had been talking, the lady had moved closer to see the zombie that had frightened her and now she stood with the dagger in her hands, trembling. With a fearful expression, she grabbed the hilt and pulled the blade from the scabbard.

"Why...? Why did this *thing* have Dustin's...?" She wailed before collapsing, tears pouring from her eyes.

Flicker knelt and gently offered her a handkerchief. "Who is Dustin? I'm sorry to ask, but could you tell us more?"

The woman nodded as she wiped at her tears. She closed her eyes to calm herself and clutched the dagger to her chest.

"I gave this to my son." She opened her eyes and withdrew the blade once more. "His name is engraved here on the metal."

"Where is he now?" Flicker asked.

"I haven't heard from him in over a year."

The silence stretched out until Flicker finally spoke again.

"Ma'am, I believe that was your son."

17

As the evening deepened, the twinkling of starlight overhead banished the foul haze, and the city tried to put itself back to normal. Under a streetlamp, Emella and her friends parted ways with Mira and Tact after extracting a promise to attend their afterparty at the Spring Flurry, a local tavern.

The little summoner set off for the Mages' Guild with Tact in tow, grumbling to herself about mandatory fun. She was so cross with herself that she failed to notice what was going on at the guild halls until she heard Tact say, "Looks like they're busy..."

She looked up with a start at the scene before exchanging a glance with the boy.

"Quite," she muttered.

Grabbing the boy's hand, Mira waded into the office through a sea of people and found a corner that seemed to be relatively quiet compared to the rest. It happened to be near the recycling bin for dungeon passes, so she took the opportunity to do her civic duty.

The moment she slipped the used pass into the slot, the box chimed and a girl's voice said, "Thank you for your cooperation and assistance."

"What in the world?" she mumbled as a tiny hologram of a girl appeared standing atop the box for a few seconds. After bowing to Mira, she vanished. This left the summoner to wonder if this was a work of ethereal magic or if it was a product of Solomon's technomancy.

Tact took a more practical approach and began peering into any slot or opening in search of the missing palm-sized girl.

"Oh, Miss Mira!" a voice rang out, and she turned to see Eurica holding some documents and walking her way.

"Ah. It's you," Mira said after taking a moment to recognize who was approaching.

"Did you already visit the Ancient Temple?"

"Hrmm, yes. That business is all wrapped up, so I figured I should recycle the pass."

"Oh, well, thank you. May I ask who the child is?" Eurica asked with a glance at Tact, who was still investigating the recycling bin.

"I met him yesterday, and he says he wants to be a summoner! I understand the guild gives some sort of aptitude test for that. Can we have that done here?"

"My name is Tact, and I want to be strong like Miss Mira!" Tact gave Eurica a bow, his face set in a look of determination.

"Well, hello, Tact. I'm Eurica. It's a pleasure to meet you," she said with a gentle smile. "As a friend of Miss Mira's, I am sure we can get this sorted out quickly if you'll just give me a moment; Miss Mira and I have a little business to attend to first."

It took Mira a moment to realize what Eurica was talking about.

"Ah, yes. You mentioned some other paperwork or something?" she asked, wondering if she'd been told what it was and simply forgotten. "Hrmm, very well. So long as I'm here, we might as well get it over with."

"If you'd just come this way, please." Clutching some papers, Eurica pushed through the crowd still assembled in the building. Mira took Tact's hand once more and followed along.

She led them behind the counters, then up the steps to the guild leader's office. With a brief smile to indicate that they'd arrived, she raised a hand and rapped lightly on the door.

"I've brought Miss Mira as requested, sir."

"Oho, is that so?" came a voice from inside. "By all means, show her in."

Eurica stepped aside from the slightly cracked door and then bent over so she could speak to Tact, face-to-face. "While Miss Mira has her talk, you come with me. We'll see about getting that aptitude test done."

Tact seemed ready to burst with excitement, then looked to Mira to make sure he was allowed to go on alone. She gestured to Eurica with her free hand and nodded.

"This might take a while; go ahead," she said, untangling her fingers from his grip.

"All right!" Tact quickly moved to take Eurica's hand instead, and Mira watched the two go off down the corridor to assess his magical potential.

Opening the door to the office, she called, "You wanted to see me?"

Leoneil was polishing his glasses and waved the cloth in her direction as she entered. A moment later, he had them perched back on his nose. He looked her up and down, gesturing to the seats by the coffee table. Before she could even sit, an attendant entered from a side door and began laying out cakes and tea. From the looks of it, Leoneil or his staff had taken notes on Mira's favorites.

"You look to be in high spirits," he said with a smile as he retrieved two items from his desk and made his way to join her. "Well, first off, these are for you."

Popping a piece of cake into her mouth, Mira glanced over and saw a black card and a sealed envelope in his hand.

"What's this? Solomon's doing, no doubt," she mumbled through her bite of cake as she placed her fork next to her plate and picked up the card. It was black and smooth as glass, and had strange sigils etched on the back.

"That pass will allow you to enter the restricted areas."

"Restricted areas?" Mira questioned with a suspicious glance.

Leoneil had anticipated the question, and he reached beside his chair to retrieve a map of the Schmegoffe region and surrounding islands. They'd once been a zone in *Ark Earth Online*.

Placing a finger on a symbol, he asked, "Have you heard of dungeons called the Devils' Labyrinths?"

"Hrmm. I've heard of them," Mira said noncommittally. This situation smelled of more work—the Devils' Labyrinths had a reputation for dropping good loot but being a pain to clear.

The Devils' Labyrinths were dungeons governed by a unique set of rules. Danblf had practically lived there for a while, so it stood to reason he'd have mentioned it to Mira.

Leoneil nodded at Mira's terse answer. "Good. That'll make this easier, then. It's always been a...*different* sort of place, but its eccentricities have been increasing. We've been forced to classify them as a special restricted area."

"Eccentricities? What do you mean?"

The Devils' Labyrinths were quite different compared to standard dungeons. All the enemies in the dungeon were stronger subspecies of other monsters. The chests and bosses in the deepest reaches of the dungeons would sometimes carry extremely rare items bearing the name of devils themselves—hence the players' nickname for them.

Why the strong monsters? Why the special equipment? These were the primary mysteries surrounding the dungeons, but if the guild leader was saying something had been "increasing," he must have been referring to something else.

"It seems that after a certain amount of time has passed after being looted, the treasure in its vaults is...replenished."

"So wha—I mean, oho... Well, now, that *is* interesting."

It had seemed to be the most obvious and uninteresting statement in the world...or rather in the *game*. But the days were gone when players simply waited for a dungeon to respawn so they could run it again.

When Mira's party had descended into the Ancient Temple earlier that day, monsters still dropped loot, but the massive chest at the dungeon's end no longer contained any treasure at all. If there was a dungeon still behaving like that, then it was interesting indeed.

"So you're saying...there's some issue surrounding these reappearing treasures?" Mira asked, immediately hatching a scheme to farm the loot and reap boundless profits.

"Of course Danblf's pupil would immediately hit upon the issue." Leoneil nodded, oblivious to her ulterior motives. "Just so. Once the word spread, adventurers flocked to the dungeon. More lives were lost in fights over treasure than were lost clearing out the monsters. The situation got so out of hand, we had to make the area almost entirely off-limits."

Leoneil grimaced and traced a spot on the map, a dense forest on Alcait's southwestern frontier.

"This is the Primal Forest, and that pass will allow you entry to it and the Devils' Labyrinths. I had to pull a few strings to get it done, but when the king asks..." His words seemed to begrudge the chore, but his eyebrows were piqued with interest.

"You don't seem too broken up about it, though."

"Oh, no, no! I requested a little favor in return," he said with a smile. "Always good to have the king owe you one."

"Hopefully nothing too big. He's got a lot on his plate at the moment." She put down the card and picked up the sealed envelope. "And this?"

She held the envelope up to the light and peered at it, but the paper was too thick to make anything out.

"Arrived just this morning via dragon post and addressed to you. Sent by someone named Lily. Do you know her?"

After a moment of consideration, the name rang a bell. Lily had been her designated maidservant back at the palace.

A shiver ran down Mira's spine. "Hrmm, I-I know her."

"Well! I'd be interested to meet the woman who could elicit such a reaction from the pupil of Danblf himself," Leoneil said with a good-natured smirk.

Mira had no idea why Lily would go through the trouble of sending her a sealed letter—but it couldn't be good. At least it wasn't another box of gothic lolita clothing. She chucked the letter into her Item Box and resolved to read it later.

"Changing topics. Demons." Mira eyed Leoneil to observe his reaction. She got a raised eyebrow.

"It seems you've seen something," he said after a moment of silence—his tone was concerned, but not surprised.

"There was a demon on the sixth level of the Ancient Temple," she said, taking another bite of cake and washing it down with some tea. The guild leader had asked her to scout the dungeon, and she saw no better time to make her report.

"Really?" he asked with a worried look. "A demon? Not a Lesser Demon, but an actual, full-on demon?"

"A third-ranked count at that."

Leoneil's jovial nature was banished by the news. He knew

what his intelligence network was hearing—but those had just been rumors. Now there was little doubt that the corrupt entities that had been eradicated thirty years ago were reappearing in the world. To make matters worse, they were on his doorstep.

Perhaps some had survived?

Had the report come from any other adventurer besides Mira, Leoneil would have simply regarded it as exaggeration or false boasting. If Mira hadn't come with the king's recommendation and validation that she was Danblf's pupil, he probably wouldn't have believed her either. He might not like it, but this was a highly credible report.

"But how?" he murmured to himself, turning over recent events in his mind. "No, I see. That accounts for..."

"You seem to have some idea." Mira watched his eyes go wide and his mouth tweak into a smile.

"Ah, yes. It has to do with the ward at the Ancient Temple." He fidgeted, pointing at the air as if tracing the lines of connection between clues that had seemed unrelated until now. "Let me review—the Ancient Temple is a dungeon with only one way in and one way out. We installed the ward that controls that access point."

"Indeed," Mira mumbled through another bite of cake.

"Demons can't just walk through the wards—but the demon *was* there. So how did it get in?"

"Hrmm, the ward *was* active." She nodded, allowing herself to be drawn into the unfolding riddle.

Leoneil noticed and reached over to pull another document

from the corner of his desk before tossing it to her. Unwilling to drop her forkful of cake, she batted at the flying papers with her off hand and knocked them onto the sofa.

"About a month ago, we had a problem with the warding system. The cause was unknown at the time, but your report is another piece of the puzzle."

Picking up the sheaf of papers, Mira checked over the information written on them. They appeared to be maintenance and inspection records for the warding system at the Ancient Temple Nebrapolis. Most of it was meaningless to her, but her eye caught on a column that listed causes of failure.

It said that an incredibly strong force had been applied to the ward from the outside.

"I don't know how tough your ward is, but that demon might have been able to breach it."

"Just so. When I read the reports, I believed them to be in error—wishful thinking on my part! A demon count would have doubtlessly been able to disable the ward on a C-Rank dungeon, but who would have thought such a monster even existed?" Then he muttered, "It makes perfect sense in hindsight."

"So we think this demon showed up a month ago?"

"That's a reasonable assumption, since that's when we first started having trouble with the ward." With arched eyebrows, Leoneil looked over the rim of his spectacles at Mira. "That also lines up with the appearance of the zombies."

He sat back and brooded over everything he knew about the situation in the light of this revelation. He muttered an occasional "I see," "but then," and "that means..." Meanwhile, Mira focused her attention on her cake and a certain sentence in the report.

Whereabouts of one investigator still unknown.

"I can't imagine the zombies and the demon are unrelated. Which means that the outbreak this evening must have had something to do with the demon." Gathering his thoughts, Leoneil looked out his window over the city that had been a battlefield barely an hour ago. "Quite serious indeed. Do you know the current whereabouts of the demon?"

Speculation was all well and good, but the threat needed to be addressed. And the sooner, the better. Forces would need to be mustered and an expedition mounted to neutralize the enemy.

"Dead," said Mira flatly. "He was useful as a...*test subject* for me to try out my battle skills now that...I'm no longer with Master Danblf. It, uh, always pays to see how one's skills work in the real world."

Visually relieved, Leoneil flopped back in his chair and let out a long, sighing breath. "Wonderful. Simply marvelous. I can't say that I'm entirely surprised, but at the same time, the city cannot thank you enough for that service."

Then his face clouded over, and a frown returned. "But even if we know the cause of the zombie outbreak, we still don't know the reason. I thought perhaps the zombies were searching for something, but if a demon was involved, then that hypothesis doesn't hold water."

"Hrmm. If they were searching for something, it would have

been easier to use Devil-Bats or the Ceiling-Eyes." Mira reeled off the monsters from memory. They'd been frequent summons for demons in need of scouts during in-game events. Zombies were cannon fodder at best.

"Well, whatever the reason, that doesn't explain that whole incident this afternoon. It was very different from the actions of the zombies we've observed before. They'd been worrisome but nonviolent."

As Leoneil continued to ponder the hidden truth behind the incursion, he submerged himself entirely within his own subconscious. Somewhere, there was an answer, if only he could turn every clue on edge and assemble the puzzle properly. He stared up at the ceiling, trying to think of everything in new ways.

Leaving the man to his brooding, Mira enjoyed a few more slices of cake, then quietly thanked his attendant and showed herself out of the guild leader's office.

She Professed Herself Pupil of the Wise Man

18

"Now where did those two get off to?" Mira mumbled to herself as she looked down the seemingly endless hallway lined with unmarked wooden doors.

After a few moments, she used her Biometric Scan to search the surrounding area. There were pings everywhere, and Tact was impossible to pick out from the crowd.

After a quick look around, she gave up and headed back downstairs. Sooner or later, Tact and Eurica would have to pass through the lobby.

The first-floor hall was calmer than it had been when they arrived. She let herself daydream as she walked, imagining what Tact might be like as an apprentice and how much she might teach the lad as he walked the path to becoming a summoner. What items should she give him? What spirit would they target to forge his first summoning contract? How would it be different from when she was a novice and just starting the game?

Lost in thought, she made her way through the front hall and bumped into several people without seeming to notice.

Finally, she found a seat in the corner, sat down, and took stock of her surroundings. She couldn't understand why she was being stared at by half the people in the office.

"Hrmm...what's with all the attention?" she muttered, before deciding that now would be a good time to trade one source of anxiety for another. Reaching into her Item Box, she withdrew Lily's letter and opened it. The envelope only held one sheet of paper, and on it was written:

Something I forgot to mention.
F – 2117, 9, 20
L – 2126, 8, 11
K – 2132, 6, 18
A – 2138, 1, 14
D – 2146, 5, 12

Mira stared at the paper quizzically. It contained nothing else but Solomon's signature scrawled on the lower right-hand corner—his real signature, not the royal signature. It was a mark only she would recognize.

Hrmm. So it wasn't from Lily at all...but what the blazes does this code mean?

Sitting with the letter on her lap, she sipped at an apple au lait. This was some sort of cipher, and she figured that her brain needed more sugar to be effective—the cake she'd eaten in Leoneil's office was beginning to wear off.

Letting out a sigh, she checked to see if Tact and Eurica had appeared yet. They hadn't, but she caught sight of a grandfather clock positioned on the opposite wall of the guild hall. Beside it hung a calendar, with the pages flipped open to the current month and a whimsical picture of a kitten.

I don't know if I'm ever going to get used to modern things in a fantasy setting. Mira frowned.

But as she looked at the calendar, the numbers in the letter suddenly made sense. They were dates.

The current date was May 19th, 2146, and Mira had arrived on May 12th. Next to that date, Solomon had scrawled a "D." She reasoned that it stood for Danblf.

Flonne, Luminaria, Kagura, Artesia, and myself. Solomon mentioned checking his friends list every day, so if they aren't listed here, they must have arrived before him.

Normally, the date alone wouldn't help, but the Nine Wise Men she was searching for were...*conspicuous.* If any noteworthy events happened on or just after those dates, it was highly likely that they were somehow connected to her targets.

With that in mind, she turned back to the initials.

She glared at the paper for a while before deciding to ask Leoneil if she could pick through his records to see what she might find. But as she stood, Eurica led Tact down the stairs and into the front hall.

"Ah, there you are." Eurica smiled as she spotted Mira. "We checked everywhere else but here. Funny how that always happens!"

"I've been waiting for you!" Mira said brightly. "So what's the news?"

Eurica withdrew a piece of paper from a folder and presented it to Mira. With a noncommittal smile, she said, "Here're the results."

Mira let her gaze drop down to the summary at the bottom. "Nothing for summoning, huh?"

Mira was crestfallen, looking like she was the one who had just failed a test. Tact had potential for three schools of magic—sorcery, holy magic, and divination—but her daydreams of having an apprentice were destined to stay just that.

"Well...these are all just disciplines that have formalized training programs," Eurica quickly added. "His mana reserves are much higher than the average. You have a shining future ahead of you, Tact!"

"Can I still be like you, Miss Mira?" Tact asked, his enthusiasm suddenly tempered by the shift in Mira's mood.

"Hrmm. Put the work in, and you'll be a splendid mage one day," she said with a resolute nod. Tact's smile grew wider. Then she said to Eurica, "Thanks for the help. I appreciate it."

"Oh, no, not at all. I'm happy to assist Danblf's pupil in any way that I can!" Eurica offered her hand for another shake, which seemed to be her preferred method of payment when it came to Mira.

Business complete, they left the guild hall. Mira stared out at the streetlights as she tried to remember the name of the tavern where the others were holding the post-adventure party.

What was it called again? The Spring...something or other.

Unable to quite remember, she took Tact's hand and stepped out into the bustling nightlife on the main street.

While there had been a concerted effort to clean up, the signs of the earlier zombie invasion still remained. The Knight Patrol walked the streets in force, keeping an eye on the scattered piles of corpses.

One such patrolman noticed two unaccompanied children walking the streets well after dark and approached to see what was amiss.

"Good evening. What are you two doing out at this hour?" he asked with a smile.

"Hrmm? What?" said Mira as she gave up her search for the tavern and turned to see who was addressing her.

Tact bowed politely to the armored man in a blue-and-white tabard. "Good evening, Mr. Officer."

"Sorry if I surprised you. I'm Corporal Ewin, Knight Patrol. Can I ask you for your names?" It seemed that the police were police, no matter what world she was in.

"My name is Tact," he replied quickly.

"I'm Mira," came her customary response, but more slowly than usual, as she was unsure what the problem seemed to be.

"Tact and Mira." Corporal Ewin withdrew a notepad and took down their names for his report. "So what are you two doing out so late? Are you lost? I can walk you both home."

Ewin had a reassuring smile, and finally Mira understood what was going on. She fought to disguise her cringe as she realized she was being mistaken for a lost child.

"We're not lost," she huffed. Then, realizing that the man was just doing his job, she added, "But we do have friends waiting for us at a tavern around here. The Spring something-or-other. Do you know it?"

"Ah, I see. Hmmm... There's the Wellspring, the Springtail, the Spring Flurry..."

"Oho, that's the one! That's the name of the place!"

"Well, then," Ewin said with a charming smile, just before he reached down and snatched Mira's free hand. "That's not too far from here. Allow me to escort you."

Stunned by the sudden and deliberate action, Mira couldn't even find the words to protest. Furthermore, his effusive aura of virtue made it impossible for her to pull herself free as he guided the wayward children along.

"Ah, Mira, there you are! Hey!" Emella had been standing by the front door waiting for the pair; she waved and Mira simply glared in return. "Huh? Did you guys get into trouble?"

"Quiet, you!"

Emella burst into laughter and stumbled back into the dining hall to tell the others. No matter how Mira tried to spin it, her denials fell on deaf ears after Corporal Ewin remanded her to Emella's care and wished the party a good evening.

"It was just a misunderstanding," Mira muttered unconvincingly, glaring up at Emella and Zef.

"Oh, sure," Emella said with sparkling eyes.

"I totally understand," said Zephard flatly. "Happens to me all the time."

"Hmm, very good." Mira narrowed her eyes at the pair. Their faces twitched, but they managed to suppress their comments and laughter.

Emella and Zef both nodded in agreement. Mira's expression relaxed, completely oblivious to the fact that the two were desperately trying to restrain themselves.

"Anyway, come on, Mira!" said Emella. "Everyone else is waiting inside."

The first floor of the tavern was a wood-framed atrium. A number of simple but sturdy-looking tables and chairs seated a few customers here and there, all seeming to enjoy a few minutes of normalcy after the chaos of the evening.

Asval waved from his seat at a larger table in one corner of the dining area and called, "Oho, little miss and master, we've been waiting for you!"

"This way, Mira," said a familiar voice, and the summoner tensed up. Like a cat stalking its prey, Flicker had moved in behind her to snatch her hand and drag her toward two empty seats at the table.

She arranged Mira in one of the chairs, but as she went to sit in the other, her cunning plan met a roadblock in the form of an elven swordswoman who'd already sat down. Emella smiled at Flicker and pointed at a seat across the table, much to Mira's relief.

Undeterred, Flicker quickly made to sit in the vacant seat on the other side of Mira, only to find Tact sliding into the chair. With a defeated look, she crossed to the other side and flounced down into the empty seat between Asval and Zephard.

Emella spread a menu before Mira and Tact as Asval called for a waiter. "Why don't we start with drinks? What would you like, Tact?"

"I'd like an orange juice, please."

Asval smiled, and when a waiter appeared, he was the first to order a large beer. Emella, Flicker, and Zef followed suit before Mira ordered two orange juices.

As soon as the waiter confirmed their order and left, Zef got down to brass tacks.

"Time to divvy up the loot," he said, spreading sixty-four Mobility Stones and the Mobility Crystal across the table while giving Mira a pointed look. "I'll ask one last time: are you sure you're all right with this?"

Mira rolled her eyes. "I thought that matter was settled."

"I know, but..." Emella shifted uncomfortably in her seat, torn between the riches on the table and a sense that she hadn't properly earned them.

Zephard simply nodded to Mira and started counting out the stones into five equal piles.

"Our vice captain's principles would keep us in the poor house," said Asval with a grin as he scooped his share into a pouch. "Can't say I disagree, but a man's got to eat."

"Thanks for waiting." The cheerful voice of the waiter broke in as he delivered their drinks and scurried off.

"Let's start with a toast," Asval said as he hoisted his mug.

Everyone took their beverages in hand and turned toward Mira.

"Hrmm...what now? You want me to do it?" Mira had always left such things to others, both in the game and in real life.

"You were the star of the show today, Mira," Zef said with a smile, waggling his glass impatiently.

"Well, If I must." Raising her glass in response to their stares, she puffed herself up and decided to toast the best news of the day. "To Tact, who showed aptitude for sorcery, holy magic, and divination!"

"Cheers! Wait, what?!" Flicker nearly forgot to take a drink as the news sunk in.

"Ha! Well done! Cheers!" called Asval, who then drained his mug.

"To Tact! Cheers!" Emella took a much more modest pull from her glass.

"Ah...umm. Thank you very much!" said Tact with a wide grin.

Amid the excitement, Zef waved lightly to a figure who approached the table.

"This sure seems lively," said a young man wearing a simple burgundy vest. He was tall, with long red hair and a slightly androgynous appearance. If not for his voice, he could've easily been mistaken for a lady. "So I take it that this is the pupil?"

"Yep, that's Mira," replied Flicker exuberantly, "and the boy next to her is Tact."

With a polite nod of his head, the man introduced himself, "I'm Cyril, Captain of the Écarlate Carillon. I owe you a debt for taking good care of my guildmates."

"No thanks necessary. It's always more fun to travel with a party," Mira replied.

"Well, that's good to hear." He smiled at her words.

"Mira! You think so much of us?" Emella had worried that they'd been no help at all. She was touched by the kind words.

"I had fun too!" said Flicker, climbing up from under the table to sit on Mira's lap and dote on the small summoner.

"Wha?!"

Mira kicked her legs in shock, unseating the mage just before she landed a solid blow to Flicker's solar plexus. The purple-clad mage slid to the ground, groaning in pain with a smile of satisfaction plastered across her face.

"I do hope that Flicker wasn't too much of a bother on your journey?" Cyril asked with a wry grin.

"She was quite a pest," Mira said, looking down at the lecherous heap at her feet.

"I'm so sorry."

"Don't worry about it. Nothing I can't handle."

"So are these the spoils from today's adventure?" Cyril asked, looking over the stones still on the table. "That's quite the haul."

"Mostly thanks to Mira," Emella added quickly. "But she says we're all splitting it equally. Isn't that generous?"

"Really now? And a Mobility Crystal too... Easily worth a million, a million and a half ducats altogether." Cyril gave Mira an appraising look. "That's a year's salary for most folks. Or a few months of lavish spending. And I understand there's a weapon as well?"

"That's right, the scythe. It belonged to, well...you-know-who. Anyway, Mira says we should give it to Kilic."

"A scythe? My, where did you get that from?"

"Uh..."

Before Cyril's line of questioning could proceed, Emella pulled the scythe from her Item Box, and it dropped to the floor with a resonant thud.

"Well...that's ominous," Cyril said as he grasped the handle of the jet-black scythe.

And despite his willowy physique, he hoisted it up one-handed—and *that* got Mira's full attention. Just what sort of stats did Cyril have? While he was distracted with the scythe, she focused on him and used her Inspect skill.

"Hrmm?!"

Nothing.

Her skill didn't work on him. Had she encountered another former player?

"What's wrong, Mira?" The sound of surprise that escaped her lungs did not escape Flicker's ears.

"Hrmm? Oh, you're still here. It's nothing. I was just surprised by how easily he lifted the scythe."

What were the customs regarding former player interaction in this world? It was something that she hadn't thought to ask Solomon. For now, she decided to leave the matter alone until she knew more.

"That's our captain for you. A league apart!" Asval boasted. "Even the pupil of the legendary Danblf has to admit he's something special."

"No, no, I'm not that special." Cyril chuckled humbly. "But enough about me. This is quite the weapon."

"That's part of what makes it so hard to deal with," said Mira.

"Given the good character displayed by your guildmates, I felt it wouldn't be used for evil if left in your hands. So if you know someone who could put it to good use, give it to them."

"Sound reasoning..." With a wicked smile, he continued, "But if I may ask, are you sure you can trust us so freely? What if we've played you for an easy mark?"

"Well, then, I'd say I've been played. Our time together has been short, but I've grown fond of this bunch," chuckled Mira. Then an idea struck her, and she stared directly into his eyes as she added, "Call it...*lending faith*."

Lending faith. An old game expression for the habit of lending an expensive item to party members with the implicit faith that the item would be used to strengthen the party and not sold for a quick profit.

"Thank you for *lending faith* to my comrades," Cyril responded with a knowing nod. "I'll take full responsibility for this."

"Please see that you do."

The other members of Écarlate Carillon watched the exchange between the two with apprehension before heaving a relieved sigh. They were out of their depth when it came to this exchange, but they knew an understanding had been reached.

As Mira reminded them that this was supposed to be a party, they pulled up a chair for Cyril and ordered another round.

She
Professed
Herself
Pupil of the
Wise Man

19

THE CONVERSATION STARTED with Emella and Mira's first encounter, and from there, the story continued on. By the time the food arrived, the retelling had progressed as far as the Ancient Temple.

Zef waxed on about how Alfina was just his type, while Emella lamented that her borrowed spirit blade had barely seen any action. Meanwhile, Asval joked that the gap between Mira's appearance and her actual abilities was better described as a canyon. Whenever she could, Flicker tried to scooch closer to Mira in hopes of getting another hug.

Mira watched them enjoy themselves, feeling a little envious at how obviously they adored Cyril.

Occasionally, they'd entreat her for some backup to whatever story they were telling with a "Right?" or a "Don't you think?" and she'd always reply with an absentminded "Indeed." The only thing she rebuffed were Flicker's advances.

Given the madness of the past few weeks, she found herself enjoying their company. There was something peaceful and mundane about listening to their happy conversation, periodically wiping food from Tact's face, and ordering more drinks.

As the post-adventure party wound down, the attention turned from the food to the drink, and the conversation turned from the temple to the zombies.

"A shocking way to get welcomed home, that's for sure." Zef chuckled around a mouthful of fries as he thought back to just a few hours earlier.

"It surprised me as well," said Cyril, who had been coordinating defense. "I have no idea what caused it. But what was a bigger shock was the sudden appearance of those seven Valkyries."

He cast an interested gaze toward Mira.

"Wasn't that great? I tell you, I'd take summoning over necromancy any day." No one was sure if Zef was talking about the battle applications or the potential of having an ideal harem on call.

After an awkward pause, the conversation continued on for a while before returning to the subject of what to do with the loot. The Mobility Stones were easy enough to divvy up equally; the Mobility Crystal less so. After some talk about selling it and splitting the profit, Emella proposed just giving the gem to Mira. The rest of the party readily agreed to the idea, and the matter was settled.

That left the matter of the demon parts, and Zef thankfully had the good sense not to pile them on the tabletop in a public tavern. They quietly agreed to figure out what to do with those items a little later.

As the party continued, the sound of the bell above the door pulled Asval's attention and he found himself looking at a familiar face.

"Oh, if it isn't Kilic! Perfect timing!"

Wearing dull black armor and an expressionless face, Kilic was a tough person for Mira to get a read on. But as Asval called his name, the ghost of a smile flickered across his face. The difference in expression was so slight, it would be impossible to tell without comparing photographs, but Asval immediately recognized that Kilic was in a good mood.

"What are you up to, Asval?" he asked in a monotone voice. "Perfect timing for what?"

"We've got a little present for you." Asval grinned, then shot a glance to Mira as if to ask, "You're certain you want to do this?"

Mira began to nod in assent, before Kilic caught sight of her and recoiled.

"Adorable..." he muttered too quietly for anyone to hear.

Realizing that she was the subject of his gaze, she panicked briefly before covering it with a cough that caused her to choke on her bite of tart.

"You must be the dark knight they mentioned," she said after the coughing fit subsided. She tried to regain a dignified tone, but that was undone by some cream stuck to the corner of her mouth.

"That is correct, I am a dark knight... Asval, what's going on?"

"You're a lucky man, that's what." The big warrior waggled his finger and rose to his feet to clap Kilic on the shoulder. Then he gestured to Cyril, and the guild captain rose and presented Kilic with the scythe.

"What?! I can feel a great flame hidden within...but what's the meaning of this?" The normally stoic dark knight struggled to keep his composure while inspecting the unique weapon.

"Little miss here says she doesn't need it, so she asked us to give it to someone who could use it. You're the only one in our guild who could wield it—so it's yours. Go on, give it a heft. Think you can use it?"

Kilic repressed a shudder as he felt the energy flowing through the scythe. He took a step back and grasped the handle of the weapon in both hands.

"There's a wild power inside...but I think I can tame it," he answered as he slowly felt the scythe grow familiar in his hands.

"Oho, it looks good on you," Mira said, smiling in satisfaction.

Asval nodded. "What do you think, little miss? I'll vouch for his character. He may look gloomy, but he donates to orphanages and delivers meals to the elderly."

"How do you know about that?!" Kilic nearly dropped the scythe in panic. He had not been as sneaky as he believed.

"Come on, everyone knows about it," Zef teased with a smile. The other guild members present all nodded in agreement.

"Very well," Mira interjected, trying to take some of the pressure off the dark knight. "You...Kilic, was it? I'm entrusting you with the scythe. Be diligent, and always act in the service of good."

His expressionless mask crumpled as he blushed, further convincing Mira that he was the right choice.

"See, Kilic? Doesn't it feel nice to be recognized?" Emella asked sweetly.

"Hmph... I can tell just by holding it that this is no ordinary scythe. Are you sure I can have this?"

"Use it for the benefit of the world and for others—that's all I ask." Mira looked him straight in the eyes as she replied.

"I assure you I won't do anything to put me at odds with that. Thank you." Then Kilic bowed deeply to the seated party...and didn't rise.

"Ahem! Hrmm. You're...welcome?" Mira mumbled, then nibbled at her tart to cover her embarrassment. She was greatly relieved when he took that as a cue to stand back up.

"It feels wrong to just accept something like this. Is there anything I can do for you in return?" he asked with a serious expression after carefully depositing the scythe into his Item Box.

"A favor, eh?" Mira pondered the offer. She'd expected nothing—but she couldn't deny that her task list kept growing longer by the day.

"That's right. As the captain of the guild, I would like to offer my thanks. You've done us several good turns in short order."

"Hrmm," Mira placed a finger to her chin to find the dollop of cream stuck there. Wiping it away, she continued, "Well, if you're going to insist, there is something I might ask of you."

"Of course, leave it to us." Cyril nodded immediately.

"Perhaps you'll live to regret that offer." Mira smiled wryly as she withdrew the envelope from her Item Box. "You asked for adventure, and I have nothing but paperwork to offer! I have a few dates here, and I'd like you to investigate to see if there were any incidents—accidents or unusual goings-on—on those days or the weeks that followed them. What do you think? Can you do it?"

"Information gathering, is it? We do have a few members skilled in espionage, so that shouldn't be an issue." Cyril pulled out a pen and notepad from his pocket and copied the dates as Mira repeated the numbers.

"That's it. I don't care how trivial the events may seem. If it's out of the ordinary, then I want to know about it." She slipped the paper back into its envelope and returned it to her Item Box.

Closing his notebook and then doing likewise, Cyril replied, "Our guild members are the best in the business. I'll get them on the case. I don't know why these dates are significant, but I promise to keep whatever we find confidential."

"That would be appreciated."

Solomon might not have intended for her to outsource any of the tasks included in her mission. But when he had asked her to locate the rest of the Wise Men within a year, he should have known that she couldn't do it all on her own. Besides, having a private guild do some of the work was still more discreet than having the Alcaitian Army or other state agents running around the countryside in search of the missing mages.

With that issue concluded, the talk returned to light chatter until the tavern's clock struck nine. As she listened to the gentle tolling of the bell, Mira checked her own watch.

"Already this late? Tact, what time did you tell your grandfather you'd be returning?"

"It's fine," Emella said. "We were going to spend the night in the Ancient Temple. His grandad's not expecting him back until tomorrow. Right, Tact?"

Despite her words, Tact seemed fidgety. Up until that point, he'd been enjoying himself, but now he refused to meet anyone's gaze.

"Tact," Mira said slowly, "you *did* tell him that you were going to the Ancient Temple, right?"

The boy jolted and his face turned red.

Mira sighed and then looked Tact in the eyes. "Tact, my boy—you weren't the only one hurt by the news of your parents' apparent death. Your grandfather must have grieved just as much."

"I know..."

"Do you want him to worry about you as well? Are you trying to trouble your grandfather?" As she lectured him, Tact silently shook his head side to side. "Of course not. But from now on, you need to tell him where you're going when you go out. Promise me, all right?"

"All right." He nodded as Mira hugged him.

"That's a good boy," she said, and he was reminded of his mother's warmth, which had seemed a distant memory.

"Mira is so adorable when she's big-sisterly..."

"Don't ruin this," Emella growled as her free hand lashed out to restrain Flicker, whose gaze had turned hungry.

Zephard narrowed his eyes and murmured, "I don't want to sound like Flicker, but Mira seems to be older than she looks at times..."

"Oho, is that going to be your excuse?" Asval laughed. "And here I thought the Valkyrie sisters were more of your type."

"Whoa! Not cool, man!"

The commotion attracted Cyril's attention. "Do I need to hear more about this?"

"Zef, I thought you preferred the more full-figured types?" asked Kilic earnestly.

Trying to take some of the heat off of Zephard, Mira rose and took Tact's hand. "Well, seeing as I'm the one who decided to take Tact into a dungeon, I'll be responsible for seeing him home."

"Little miss, there's still the *rest* of the loot to divvy out," Asval said with a knowing wink. "What should we do with it?"

Realizing he was referring to the remnants of the demon, Mira said, "Very well. I suppose I could return after delivering Tact."

"In that case, why don't I escort the boy?" Cyril countered. Mira suspected that he'd been briefed on the incident and he was well aware of their need for confidentiality.

"No, but..." It was a generous offer, but Mira really wanted an excuse to say her goodbyes for the evening and get back to her plush hotel room.

Just as she was about to refuse, Kilic stood as well. "I too shall accompany them. It is the least I can do after the gift I've received this evening. The child's safety is guaranteed."

There was no arguing it. With the two of them as escorts, Tact would be safe even if the zombies invaded for a second time that evening. Still, she was reluctant to agree.

"If Mira saw him home, she might get picked up by the Knight Patrol again," Emella teased.

Mira was mortified. Her head drooped to her chest, and she conceded to their offer with a resigned wave.

"Miss Mira, Miss Emella, Master Asval, Miss Flicker, Mr. Zef. Thank you all so much! I'll pay you back someday!" Tact stood up straight and tall and bowed deeply. When he straightened, his face was filled with gratitude and deep admiration. A marked difference from the weeping child whom Mira had bumped into the day before.

"See you around, Tact," Asval said with a wave and a smile.

"When you become an adventurer, give me a holler. I'll teach you a thing or two."

"And if you choose to be a sorcerer, I might be able to teach you something as well," Flicker added. "Feel free to ask anytime."

"Master...huh?"

The rest of the group gathered around and patted Tact on the head. The well-pampered boy could only squeeze out another "All right!" with a boyish smile.

"Hmm, well, now... Make sure to let your grandfather know that your parents are still alive," Mira instructed. "I'm sure he'll be happy to hear it. And you've got three options in becoming a mage. The choice is yours. Whichever you choose, make sure to pay a visit to the Linked Silver Towers. There's a welcome waiting for you... Just be sure to talk it over with your grandfather first."

"Yes, ma'am!" Tact glanced around the room once more, as if to firmly imprint the image of the moment in his mind. The memory would last a lifetime.

As soon as the boy was out the door, Flicker could no longer restrain herself. "Mira! What about *my* invitation to the Linked Towers?!"

The Linked Silver Towers were the largest institute of magical research on the entire continent, not just inside Alcait. The towers were a den of single-minded madmen intent on expanding their disciplines at all costs. Even top-tier adventurers might find themselves turned away at the gate.

As the *pupil* of Danblf, Elder and highest-ranking member of the Tower of Evocation, Mira had access that others didn't. Given the battle they'd witnessed in the depths of the Ancient Temple, it was clear that she could earn a place within the Towers. By offering a blanket invitation to Tact, she had unknowingly flaunted her influence in front of her lecherous and jealous compatriot.

"Mira! Just get me in to have a look! I'm begging yooou!" Flicker groveled and clutched at Mira's boots—yet the sorceress was looking at her for the first time with something other than lust. Her eyes were filled with a mage's thirst for knowledge.

"Fine, fine! When I have the time, I'll show you around. Just let me go!"

"I love you, Mira!" With Mira's acquiescence, Flicker's personality flipped once again and she pounced, only to be intercepted by Emella.

Dinner and drinks finished, the group retired to Zef's room on the second floor of the tavern.

"All right, now for the truly interesting stuff." Zephard spread the demon parts out across the table. There were two twisted horns, eight gleaming black claws, a stretch of jet-black hide that had survived the fire, and the two wings.

All of them seemed to have a corrupted aura about them, and Emella had the sinking suspicion that they might be cursed. But Flicker, their expert in such matters, said nothing. If there were a problem, then the lecherous mage would have spoken up.

"You look at them laid out like this and...it's just amazing." Asval sighed as he stared at the demon remains.

"The magical power in these claws alone is incredible," said Flicker. "They seem to be attuned to elemental fire. If we used them to make magical armaments, they'd be unbelievably powerful."

She picked up one of the claws, inspecting it as though searching for something.

"A flaming sword!" Emella gasped to herself, her fear of curses evaporating as her eyes twinkled in anticipation. She looked at the claws arranged on the table, then whispered, "Eight magic swords..."

"O-okay," said Zef, looking at the vice captain with a wary eye. "First things first. How do we divide them? Mira, you're sure we should split these as well? It's not like we did much besides watch the fight."

Emella groaned and the light faded in her eyes. The rest of the party knew that Mira had carried the raid.

"How many times do we have to rehash this conversation?! If you're still that bothered, just remember that your guild now owes me a favor. I need that information, and if this is the payment, then that's fine with me. I don't need demon claws—I *need* the facts about those dates."

Zef and Asval exchanged glances and shrugged.

"I would help with that no matter what, because I love you," said Flicker quietly enough that no one heard.

"Then leave it to us!" Emella said confidently, as the vision of flaming swords danced in her head.

"How about this, little miss: you take what you like, and then we'll split the rest between us."

"Hrmm, fine. If that's what it takes." Mira glanced over the table.

The hide was best suited to make armor—so it was largely useless to her. The claws were useful for mage equipment or tools, of which she had plenty. The wings were a defensive material.

She didn't need any of those. The horns, on the other hand... "I suppose I'll take these. And the rest is yours to do with as you see fit."

"You sure, little miss?" asked Asval. "Don't hold back on our account. Any one of these is a great reward from our point of view."

Demonic materials were a very rare and expensive commodity, especially since demons had been an extinct species until recently. The only demon parts still in circulation were bits and pieces from the great war over thirty years ago. What lay before them was in excellent condition compared to what might occasionally be unearthed from an old battlefield. The price would be astronomical.

"This is enough," Mira said, mulling over what she might be able to do given a quality refining table and some time to work.

"Well, you heard the lady. Now let's divvy up the rest of this lot," said Zef, looking down at the table just in time to see a hand reach out and snag a demon's claw. "Oh, Vice Captain..."

Emella found herself the target of three cold stares. "But... *swords*," she mumbled.

After several rounds of choosing and swapping, Emella wound up with five claws, Asval most of the hide, Flicker the wings, and Zef three claws and the remainder of the hide.

"Well, I suppose it's time for me to head back. This was all quite entertaining," Mira said. The other four members present stood and bowed to her. She looked at the four of them quizzically, surprised by their sudden action.

"It's thanks to you that we're still alive. I offer you my gratitude. Thank you." A smile bloomed across Emella's face like a flower, but her eyes shone with a conviction to grow stronger.

"Thank you, little miss. For everything, even this little souvenir," said Asval, smiling pleasantly as he patted his portion of the demon's hide.

"Thank you for everything, Mira. I'll make it up to you someday. So if you could just tell me how to contact you..."

Flicker was cut off by Emella's strike, allowing Zef to cut in. "Thanks to you, I was able to come to peace with a few things. Thank you."

Mira's cheeks began to burn as she was once again forced into the center of everyone's attention and praise. She looked down at her feet and a hesitant smile crept across her face.

"What's all this? I told you all thanks weren't necessary."

The cuteness was overpowering, and like a shot, Flicker lunged—only to fall victim to another of Emella's vicious chops.

AFTER SAYING HER GOODBYES to the others, Mira left the inn and stepped out into the streets of Karanak. The evening had deepened and the stars shone brightly above, though scarcely anyone remained outside to see them. Only the Knight Patrol was afforded that consolation as they went about their duty in the early morning hours.

"Allow me to escort you, Miss Mira," a familiar voice called out from nearby. For a moment, Mira cringed and thought she'd been collared again by Corporal Ewin.

Looking around, she saw Cyril leaned against a nearby lamp-post, casually waving to her.

"Normally, I'd decline, but there are things I'd like to discuss with you." Having an escort just to prevent another *misunderstanding* had a certain appeal.

With a nod and a smile, he abandoned his post and walked along beside her. Many of the lamps had been damaged during the attack, and the street was particularly eerie tonight, but neither

Mira nor Cyril noticed. Both seemed happy to have found a kindred spirit seemingly out of nowhere.

"Now, then, I'm sure you've already guessed the reason behind my offer to escort you," Cyril said once they'd walked far enough away from the tavern to avoid eavesdroppers. His tone was joyful, as if finding an old friend in a crowd.

"It seems you're a former player too," Mira commented. She wasn't sure if this was a wise move on her part, but the cat was already out of the bag.

"Yes, exactly! Which is why I felt we must talk."

When he smiled, Mira couldn't help but feel that despite his androgynous looks, Cyril might be quite the lady-killer.

"Well, then, let's talk."

"Miss Mira, how long have you been in this world?"

Mira pondered her response for a moment, then decided that telling the truth might be the best long-term strategy.

"Oh, about a week now."

"I knew it couldn't have been long," he murmured to himself. "Not many people—even former players—can defeat a demon count. Fewer still that I don't know about. You seem quite calm with your new circumstances. Back when I first appeared, I frantically searched for any method to return to our home world."

Mira narrowed her eyes as thoughts of her past life rose unbidden in her mind. "That doesn't seem unreasonable, given the circumstances."

A method to return home—Mira had thought about it, but she'd quickly dismissed the search as soon as she encountered

Solomon and Luminaria. Not because she was content to spend the rest of her life with her online friends, but because even those two hadn't figured a way back in the past thirty years. What was the point in her searching?

"It was thanks to my friends." They certainly had done her a good turn in getting her acclimated to the new world as quickly as they could. She smiled and casually wondered what they were up to at the moment.

"Friends, eh? I'm assuming you knew them before coming to this world. That must have helped, I'm sure," Cyril agreed.

"Indeed. Even though they've got me running errands for them at the moment."

"You're lucky to have found them within a week. It took me about a year and lots of hardship."

"That long? I was close to the towers on my arrival and already knew where to look." It was quite lucky, come to think of it. She could have appeared half a continent away and had to make her way to Alcait across potentially hostile borders.

"Towers? Do you mean the Linked Silver Towers? Ah, that's right, you're the pupil of Master Danblf. That would help."

Mira's face twitched when Cyril mentioned her *new* title. "That's the place."

As a former player himself, Cyril would have known about Danblf. She realized that if she wasn't careful with her responses, her true identity might be revealed, and any shreds of dignity she had left might be torn away forever.

"I don't remember hearing that any of the Wise Men, much

less Master Danblf, had taken apprentices... Were you two friends in real life or something?" Cyril asked. "There have been imposters over the years, but something about your story rings true. Who else would use a combination of summoning and the immortal arts?"

Mira laughed nervously. "Yep, not many ways to explain it other than that..."

"Ah, or perhaps, Miss Mira...*you're* actually Master Danblf." Cyril's smile seemed to imply that he said it as a joke, but his tone had an edge to it, and he watched her reaction with interest.

Oh, hell! He's right on the money! How do I get myself out of this?! No, calm down! He's just messing around. Should I laugh it off as a joke? Would laughing too much tip him off that I'm trying to make a production of it? Which should I do?!

With the truth dangling there between them, Mira silently pulled out an apple au lait and took a swig as she desperately tried to maintain her composure. Then, after suppressing the urge to throw a tantrum, she thought of what to say.

"No, of course not. We were indeed IRL friends. He would teach me this and that. It's not too surprising that I wasn't a big figure in-game, as my job kept me from logging in as much as I would have liked." She feigned calm in hopes that it would sell the amendment to her backstory.

"I see. That would explain it."

I...I think he bought it?

She stole a glance at his expression, but there was no obvious sign of contempt. Deciding that she'd escaped the trap, she tried to calm herself back down. Cyril cast a kind look over her, as her agitation was obvious.

Before he could ask any more questions, Mira decided it was best to turn the tables. "So with that said about my situation, what can you tell me about yourself? How does a player live in this world?"

Solomon and Luminaria obviously had unique living situations, and she was curious as to the life of a player who wasn't a king or a Wise Man.

"Hmm, let's see. Well, for starters, I appeared just ten days after the First Day."

"Hrmm, the First Day, you say?"

"You haven't heard of it yet? The First Day was the day the game became reality: September 14, 2116. It seems that no matter what day a player returns, the last day they remember of the real world is the same."

"September 14, hmm? That was the same for me." Mira dug through her memory and recalled that the email informing her to spend the rest of the funds in her account before they expired had been sent on the 13th.

She'd bought a vanity chest, stayed up all night making a new avatar, and, well...

"Even now, thirty years later, that still holds true. We were all playing on the same day, but we all reappeared at vastly different times. I wonder what causes the difference?"

"I wonder, indeed." She pondered that riddle but decided that if it hadn't been answered by anyone in the past three decades, she wasn't going to solve it on the walk back to her hotel.

"My experience entering this world isn't particularly unique. Obviously, I was confused at first—suddenly, the air I was breathing felt different, and I could smell things. A few hours later, when I was hurt in battle, the pain was unbearable. Unable to figure out what was going on, I tried to log out, but the option was gone. I panicked."

Lost in his memories, he narrowed his eyes as if staring off at something in the far distance.

"After that, I fled to a nearby village and was in a daze for a while. Nobody I knew was anywhere near. I was alone, I had no idea what to do, and then this woman just started talking to me. She wasn't a friend. She wasn't another player stuck in the same situation. She was one of the NPCs that I'd never paid any attention to before."

He carried on with his reminiscing.

"I was behaving like a crazy man. Ha! I guess we all used to behave like idiots when death just meant a respawn and none of the NPCs had any emotions beyond what was programmed into them. But I was desperate, and she gave me shelter and nursed me back to health.

"A whole year I stayed with her, helping with chores and driving off monsters that wandered into the village. This world finally started to feel *real* and not like some sort of fever dream. And if this world was real, and these people were real, then they deserved better than being villagers inhabiting monster-plagued villages.

"I started teaching the young people how to fight, so they could defend their home if anything ever happened to me. They were clumsy at first, but after a time they grew more accomplished. They *improved*. Can you imagine that—NPCs who *improve*? Soon, they weren't just fodder for monsters, but they stood on their own and defended what was theirs. After that, there wasn't a need for me to hang around. I played *AEO* as a game, and now I wanted to see what it was like as a *world*."

Cyril stopped and stared up at the night sky, smiling to himself for a few moments. Then he grinned at Mira and resumed walking down the street.

"I started that journey for my own self-satisfaction, but it was laughable how quickly I learned how the rest of this world had grown and developed, even without players running the show. The village I had been in was quite rural, but as I crossed the mountains, I found a larger town with an adventurers' guild. I nearly died of shock when I happened to bump into an old friend. I can't tell you how much that surprised me.

"My friend filled me in on how things had changed in the cities, and at once, I knew that joining the adventurers' guild was the right thing to do. So I signed up. Now I travel, and I give back. Along the way, I found friends who shared my feelings. You've already met Asval and Emella. For a while, the three of us traveled together, but gradually, others came around to our way of thinking, and our numbers have swelled. There was only one thing to do."

He smiled happily and pulled a small scarlet bell from his breast pocket while giving it a little jingle.

Mira nodded and smiled in return. "I see. Perhaps it's not for me to say, as I got lucky with having my friends close at hand, but you seem to have been quite fortunate to have met those who helped you and those who sympathized with you."

"I suppose so. It hasn't been easy, but I seem to be blessed with whom I meet." He looked in her direction and gave a knowing wink.

Mira couldn't help but smile in return. She was beginning to get a faint idea as to why Cyril was going into so much detail.

"But we could do so much more," he said. "We can only save that which is within our reach. And no matter how far or how many times we desperately reach out, we find that more slips away. It is frustrating—over and over, I have wished for a hand that can reach farther and wider."

Staring at the bell in his hand, he gave it another little jingle. Then he turned to her and looked directly into her eyes. "Miss Mira, would you join our guild?"

Hrmm, I thought so. She stopped and stared back at him beneath the glow of a streetlamp. His earnestness was painfully obvious, and his conviction was powerful.

"I'm sorry," she said, and sincerely, she was. "I have a calling that demands my attention. I can't join you."

He was a commendable man, and she wished her situation would allow her the privilege of adventuring with him and his guildmates, but the weight of Alcait was heavy on her shoulders.

"I see... I somehow knew that you would refuse. But I still had to try. I assume those issues you mention have something to do with those dates from earlier?" Still, he smiled.

"Hrmm, indeed. And I may not be joining the guild, but if I hear any cries for help during my journeys, I promise I'll do what I can. How's that?"

Cyril smiled broadly and sketched a bow to the diminutive summoner.

As they wandered down the main street reminiscing about their memories of the game, they came to a stop in front of one of the piles of zombie corpses. Even with carts hauling them out of the city all evening, the heap was still massive.

"Your assistance was appreciated today. I was very surprised by the appearance of the Valkyrie sisters," Cyril said with a tint of envy.

While his adventurers had made a valiant stand against the undead, it took the Seven Sisters to truly turn the tide.

"An easy task for someone with the power of summoning!" Her eyes shone with pride.

"As expected of Master Danblf...or perhaps his *pupil*, as the case may be."

"Hrmm, I've returned to find the state of the discipline in a dismal state. Well, that's going to change now that I'm here!" The excitement of revitalizing her beloved school of magic caused Mira to completely miss the meaning of Cyril's comment.

He smiled to himself, then sighed and gestured to the pile. "But that said, what caused all this today? The bodies were the same, made of earth and plants, but everything else about today's zombies was different. I've followed these cases for about a month now, but I've never seen anything like this before."

"I was actually discussing just that with the head of the Mages' Guild."

Mira gazed at Cyril for a moment and judged him a trustworthy ally. As they walked on, she brought him up to speed concerning her earlier conversation with Leoneil. The demon, the failure of the dungeon ward, and other anomalous events that were now seemingly connected.

Cyril was still surprised that a demon had returned but admitted that their theory was highly credible.

"You can never be too careful when it comes to a demon's plans. Perhaps this conclusion has its own hidden meaning."

As players, they knew that whenever demons were involved, most events ended in tragedy. Victory was almost never a possibility—mitigated disaster was often the best one could hope for. To make matters worse, demonic encounters seldom finished when they appeared to. Just when everyone thought the event was over, a final twist would bring more tragedy.

Perhaps the zombies running rampant that evening had been the final twist. Then again, maybe they were just the next link in a longer chain to something terrible.

With that in mind, Cyril glanced at the pile of corpses with caution. Mira regarded them with disgust.

There are a lot of them. Not even just a thousand or two thousand. It might even be as many as ten thousand.

She'd been counting the piles as they passed, but her eyes suddenly stilled. Turning back around, she looked up at the largest of the heaps.

"The effect of death on the land..." she muttered.

It was the same as her mission almost a week ago. A horde of monsters had invaded, and their corpses were left strewn across the flower gardens. Had these unfortunate creatures been created, then lured here to die for the sake of death itself?

"'The effect of death on the land?' What do you mean?" Cyril asked interestedly.

"Hrmm. This is confidential, but you should probably be aware."

Mira began by asking Cyril if he had heard of the monster incursion both in Alcait and beyond. When he responded that he had, she proceeded to explain the theories of Solomon's court mage, Joachim.

In short, land could be transformed into an undead swamp by spilling the blood of countless lives across the ground. But it couldn't just be any land—it needed to be a place of hidden power. Take somewhere that was magically special, add a mass of corpses and a mass of deaths, and it would turn into an evil place that would spawn endless waves of the undead.

Mira emphasized the validity of the theory by mentioning that the Lesser Demon who led the incursion into the flower field had cackled madly as it forced monsters to turn on themselves and fight. As a former player, Cyril knew that was a bad sign—the demon's cackle was a well-known sound that signaled all hope had been lost.

She concluded by proudly stating that the second invasion had been completely thwarted within the borders of Alcait.

"I had heard that Lesser Demons were spotted, but now it seems the situation is more dire than I'd thought."

Cyril was silent for a moment, before he appeared to make a connection between Mira's report and other rumors he'd heard.

"That's right," he said with a frown. "I think it was about two months ago. A friend was going on about seeing a Lesser Demon at the Symbios Cemetery—a mass grave site. It was unearthing piles and piles of bodies. My friend cut it down on the spot, so its motives remained a mystery. What if all these incidents involving the dead and demons are related?"

Mira's story, the friend's story, and the pile in front of them. They all had one thing in common—a lot of corpses. Staring at yet another pile of zombie bodies, Cyril had a puzzled look on his face as he debated whether to consider the events separately or together.

"What fiends these demons are. Vandalizing graves is truly repulsive."

"Indeed. What was it going to do with all the bodies after digging them up?"

The two fell silent again as they pondered the inexplicable motives of the Lesser Demons. But alas, neither had a satisfactory answer.

"Such senseless destruction," Mira said, turning her gaze from the pile to the rest of the city. The damage was severe. Even in the gloom of the night, it was apparent that it would require quite a lot of material and time to repair.

"Yes, that's true. But at least no one was killed, and all injuries seem to be minor."

"Oho, that is good to hear!"

"But there are some things that still don't make sense." Cyril began to tick items of note off on his fingertips. "First, among all these zombies, there were only six humanoids. Second, we ran searches on all six and they all matched local reports of missing persons. Third, despite the zombies running rampant, the humanoid ones didn't hurt anyone."

He paused for a moment and looked up at the sky.

"Perhaps they were just cut down before they could attack anyone," he concluded, but that answer didn't seem to satisfy him.

"The plot thickens," Mira grumbled, tracing her chin with a finger. Despite the mayhem, it seemed that the humanoid zombies' behavior had remained a constant.

"If we don't know the basis of the issue, we can't just assume that it was all just the work of the demon. Though perhaps this incident was intended to take advantage of the deaths in the same ways the Lesser Demons have been doing." Cyril did his best to interpret the information while taking the unknown into account.

"That is definitely a possibility." Mira nodded. It was logical, in any case.

"But if all this is true—with this many bodies in the city—it seems the demon succeeded in its plans. We should prepare for the worst." Cyril considered Joachim's theory, then added, "I suppose the first thing to do would be to clear away these piles before anything else happens."

"Indeed. You should advise the city to make haste."

The two looked back at the pile. The corpses were plentiful, but they had only been collected there; they hadn't truly *died* within the city. Zombies were reanimated dead—they had died somewhere else and then shambled into town later. Did they count as having lost their lives in the city? Did they even count as corpses?

Was it even a problem anymore, now that the demon had been defeated? Perhaps nothing more would come to pass.

With these thoughts filtering through her mind, Mira looked up at the sky. It was full of stars shining brightly, oblivious to her problems on the ground. Just then, a meteor flashed across the night sky, appearing and disappearing in the blink of an eye—if she'd blinked, she would never have even known that it existed.

As they neared the hotel, the pair discussed how to easily stay in contact and then returned to talking about their original world. Mira laughed as she recalled how the sign for the umbrella store had reminded her of a certain survival-horror video game. Cyril nostalgically replied that he used to try to beat the game on the hardest difficulty with nothing but a knife.

They both jumped in fright as a set of footsteps approached them from behind.

"Lady Mira."

Glancing back, she saw that the owner of the footsteps was Garrett.

And why does he look so pleased?

Confirming it was her, Garrett ran up with one arm waving wildly. His face was brighter than the stars above. It seemed that after they had parted during the commotion, he had gone frolicking around the city to his heart's content.

"It seems someone is here to collect you. I shall contact you through guild services when I've found something regarding your request."

"Hrmm, thanks for the assist." She locked eyes with Cyril as she responded before spinning and walking away. "Until next time."

"Indeed, whenever that may be." With his eyes slightly downcast, he turned and left the way they had come.

Both minds were focused on the same problem.

**She
Professed
Herself
Pupil** of **the
Wise Man**

"LADY MIRA, forgive me!"

The morning after Mira had delved into a dungeon and thwarted an attack on Karanak, Garrett prostrated himself on the floor of the hotel lobby. It seemed that the carriage would need repairs after his night of *defending* the city

"Oh well, I suppose I'll find some way to pass the time." She gave him a cold stare as she donned her coat.

Standing back up more quickly than she thought possible, he bid her off into the morning with a chipper "Take care!"

Karanak was alive and bustling. Restoration work had begun here and there, and craftsmen were coming and going as they assessed and repaired damages. Processing of the zombie piles seemed to have also started in earnest, with members of the Knight Patrol and adventurers helping to load carts to carry away the bodies.

At this rate, they should be cleared away in no time.

She aimlessly strolled along the street as she checked on the state of the city. The citizens proved to be surprisingly resilient and in good spirits.

The Valkyrie sisters were the topic on everyone's tongues. The sight of them descending from the heavens like angels, dispatching the zombies in the blink of an eye, and then vanishing had stirred the imagination of all who had seen them.

More importantly, everyone had witnessed their new attack, which was both awe-inspiring and tremendous. The art of summoning was sure to come roaring back in short order with a PR campaign like this.

Convinced that her efforts had been a success, she triumphantly made her way into the crowded Mages' Guild offices. The guild was currently issuing a special quest titled, "Help the City's Recovery Efforts." The quest remuneration itself wasn't much, but it came with an additional class-specific reward and was proving to be quite popular.

Mira paid it no heed. After a wave to Eurica, who was busy at the counter, she showed herself in and headed toward the guild leader's office. Within a few moments, she was on a couch with a selection of cakes arrayed before her, and all was right with the world.

"I see... Altering the land through the power of death, eh? That could be a possibility," Leoneil muttered as he crossed his arms and leaned back in his chair. "So you think the demon hadn't been trying to use the zombies to accomplish a task; rather, it was just gathering them for another purpose?"

It was just a hypothesis, but it was the best one she had. "I don't know for sure, but given the circumstances, we can't discount it, don't you think?"

"Indeed, and this is useful information even beyond the immediate situation. Thank you."

Mira selected a tantalizing slice of chocolate cake next while Leoneil looked on, happy that he had a connection at the bakery to keep his little informant coming back for more. Their talk shifted to the wonders of summoning and the rumors spreading through the city before Mira made her exit.

The lobby seemed even noisier than when she arrived, and the Valkyries were a common topic of discussion. She smiled, glad that her efforts were bearing fruit. Leaving the guild hall, she spotted a line of people marching along while carrying large sacks—no doubt assisting in the removal of the zombie corpses— and all of them were all discussing which of the Seven Sisters they preferred.

Boundless success! Watching them pass, Mira stepped lightly as she headed back along the main street.

Garrett must be wrapping things up by now.

It was approaching noon. She picked up some snacks from a nearby bakery to eat while on the road. As she made her way back to the hotel, she gazed around at the city of Karanak and was filled with a sense of hope.

Scattered bits of rubble lay around the road, no doubt knocked off the buildings during the commotion. But the people were undaunted, and the bustle of city life undisturbed by last night's attack. How could the demons prevail over such determination?

Just then, Mira stopped dead in her tracks.

It was a shop—the Karanak branch of Moon and Silver Towers Specialty Goods. Samples of their wares hung from the awning, and one item in particular called to her.

At last! A use for this money and freedom from the oppression of the maids!

She laughed and wondered why she hadn't thought of it before. Grabbing the item with both hands, she unfurled the robe like a victory flag. It looked like the robe Danblf wore, albeit simplified and in her size. Having achieved fashion nirvana, she checked the price tag. Labeled the Wise Man's Replica Robe, it was priced at five thousand ducats. That seemed like a reasonable ask.

Selecting the Wise Man's Replica Robe (Summoner) from among the different patterns, of course, Mira held it before her in front of the full-length mirror. Confirming the fit, she rushed to press money into the merchant's hand before hurrying back to the hotel.

The moment her suite door slammed shut behind her, she stripped off every bit of frilly, girly clothing forced onto her by the maids. Beaming, she pulled her new robe over her head and took a long look at herself in the mirror. Head to toe, left to right—then she took a half-step back and spread her arms wide.

"I am reborn!"

She cheered and struck a victory pose. After admiring her reflection in the new robe, she rolled up the hem to her knees and loosened the collar.

"Not bad... Not bad," she muttered as she smirked suggestively and toyed with her options.

Half an hour later, she was finally satisfied with her adjustments, and she left her room to check on the state of the carriage repairs.

"The repairs are complete and we can leave as soon as you like," Garrett said when she found him walking back from the carriage house. "Shall we?"

Without any particular reason to stay, and with the benefit of having Control Terminals instead of luggage, Mira jumped into the carriage.

"As you wish," came Garrett's immediate reply as he carefully closed the door behind her. He then took his position on the driver's seat.

The carriage left the stables, then pulled up to the gate to the hotel. Garrett dismounted, completed the checkout procedures, and returned to drive them out onto the main street. Gazing out the carriage window at the City of Requiem, Mira reflected on the eventful few days she'd just experienced.

Tact's wish to see his dead parents and the revelation that they were somehow still alive.

Meeting Emella and the other kind-hearted members of the Écarlate Carillon.

Finding Cyril, their captain and another former player.

Discovering clues as to the whereabouts of Soul Howl.

Battling with a demon.

The connection between the zombie uprising and said demon.

She daydreamed and let the memories melt into the scenery flowing past the window.

A few days after Mira left the city, the Adventurers' Guild Union and local Knight Patrol jointly announced an end to the zombie incident.

The official statement declared that excess undead magical energy had spilled over from the nearby Ancient Temple Nebrapolis. As a result, the site was elevated to A-Rank access and the wards were strengthened. The public was never informed that a demon had been killed in the depths of the dungeon.

The Union checked the identity of the humanoid zombies against their missing persons list. Most were identified, and the bodies were returned to their bereaved families.

Throughout the city, a rumor spread...a rumor of seven maidens, all noble, beautiful, and incredibly powerful. There was much argument as to which guild the women belonged to.

The recovery of the summoning arts might take a while longer, it seemed.

Cats, Underwear, and Firsts

NINE SPIRES rose toward the noonday sun above the Sacred City of Silverhorn, located in the southwest corner of the Kingdom of Alcait. Both the symbol of the city and the seat of magical research on the continent, the Linked Silver Towers were beloved by mages and tourists alike.

A gate situated along the high wall surrounding the tower compound allowed access to the city's main street, and it was through this gate that a fairy passed. She repeated words to herself over and over, almost like a chant. But it wasn't a magical incantation—it was a shopping list.

Mariana, attendant to the Elder of the Tower of Evocation, was on a mission to make sure Mira's next visit would be a bit less scandalous. Master Danblf had entrusted her with the care of his precious pupil, and she would not fail him.

Well, he hadn't actually said that... He'd been missing for thirty years. But it was what he would have wanted, and that was all that mattered.

Now, what should I buy first?

She pondered this and was struck by the memory of when she first met Mira, half-asleep and mostly naked.

Right, let's start with a nightgown.

She triumphantly made her way toward a shop specializing in bedwear. The sign above the door was emblazoned with the mascot of a stuffed animal that looked like a cross between a bear and a pig. "Pookey Bear" was printed below the whimsical picture, and the store specialized in all things sleep. Founded in Lunatic Lake, the establishment sold fashionable and practical goods. The Silverhorn branch was brand-new.

Inside, Mariana found a directory and located ladieswear on the second floor. The number of customers and the endless aisles of products were nearly overwhelming, but she soon found the sleepwear section and began her hunt.

Then came the difficult task of choosing. She personally preferred plain, undecorated nightgowns, but it seemed that styles for young ladies had changed radically to favor eccentric prints and lacy frills. What would Mira like? Arranging Master Danblf's treasures and keeping the quarters tidy were one thing, but selecting sleepwear for a girl she'd only met once was something else entirely.

A bit farther down the aisle, a young girl and her mother were shopping as well. The girl seemed about the same age as Mira, and after a quick look through some of the options, she picked one up and exclaimed, "This is so cute!"

"It is," her mother agreed. "I'm sure it'll look great on you. Let's go try it on."

Waiting until the pair moved away, Mariana rushed over to see what the girl had been looking at. It was a section of nightgowns sharing a similar design, but in differing sizes. Which begged a question: What size did Mira wear?

Mariana held her hands in the air, widening and narrowing them to try and remember Mira's general shape.

"Maybe something like this?" she murmured when her hands were roughly shoulder-width apart. Looking at her reflection in a nearby mirror, she realized the Mira had been almost the same size as herself. That would be handy—if she found something that fit her, then by extension, it should fit Mira as well.

The shop had everything from animal print pajamas to see-through negligees. Mariana picked one of the former, thinking it more appropriate for a girl of Mira's age. The loose-fitting pair of purple pajamas had a sleepy-looking version of the store's mascot printed on the chest.

Decision made, she took the outfit to the counter, and as the clerk rang her up, she saw the same mother and child she'd seen before. The girl was picking up all sorts of items and declaring them to be "cute" before piling them into the waiting hands of her mother.

If they were all cute, then what did *cute* even mean? Still unsure, Mariana left the bedwear store pondering a new philosophical conundrum.

Where to next?

She glanced around the main street and spotted a souvenir shop on the other side of the road.

The Sacred City of Silverhorn, a holy land to mages, was a well-known tourist attraction. Accordingly, the main street was home to a great many shops offering trinkets and keepsakes. Goods related to the Nine Wise Men were commonplace, and the shop Mariana stood before seemed to focus on apparel.

She didn't know who they would appeal to, but the products hanging from the eaves were all replicas of the Wise Men's costumes. This included replicas of the Elders' robes in both adult and child sizes, Soul Howl's favorite ominous cloak, and even Danblf's treasured rainbow loincloth.

"That's right, undergarments," she said with a nod after staring at the souvenirs for a moment. The first time they had met, Mira was missing underwear. That wouldn't do at all.

She strolled down the boulevard to the lingerie shop Litte-Lotte. Inside, the shop was airy and bright, decorated with pastel colors, with an open atrium in the center for customers to rest. Most of the clientele this morning were ladies.

Fashion on the continent was highly informed by the days when the world had been a game. The players had introduced a wide range of cultures to what should have been a classical fantasy game—and the realm of women's underwear made that cultural influx apparent.

Mariana stood and gawked at a rack of panties that looked considerably more *decorative* than she was comfortable with. For a fairy given to wearing modest drawers and slips, this was uncharted territory.

Do these even count as underwear?!

She picked up a pair from the shelf and unfolded it. "This is what they call panties?"

An impulse seized her, and she looked around to make sure she wasn't being watched. Then she held them before her hips and imagined what they'd look like on her frame.

They're pretty...but not really my style.

It was sort of like trying on jewelry, but with an extra little thrill. Unfortunately, these just weren't appropriate, and her shoulders slumped as she felt slightly dejected. Still, no matter—she had a mission to complete.

But the more she looked, the more questions she had. What was Mira's taste in underwear? There were so many styles after all. And what was fashionable? What did they keep around for people who *didn't* care about fashion? She wore a pensive look on her face as her options piled up with no clear answers.

"Oh my, if it isn't Miss Mariana. What an unusual place to bump into you," a familiar voice called.

"Oh, Miss Lythalia. Good morning. What a...*coincidence.*" As she bowed to her counterpart and friend, she caught sight of the bag Lythalia was carrying.

"Do you shop here often?" she asked the elven assistant to the Tower of Sorcery.

"Oh, this shop is one of my favorites," Lythalia said, looking as if she'd been dying for Mariana to ask. "I've been coming here ever since it opened."

A wave of calm swept over Mariana—her savior had arrived.

"Oh, that's excellent! I need your assistance." The fairy

reached out and grabbed Lythalia's free hand with a pleading look in her eye. "This is my first time here, and I have no idea what I'm doing."

"Well, now, you don't say? Of course I'll help." That was just who Lythalia was. Besides, it would be fun using her friend as a dress-up doll for a bit. "Now then, what is it that you're looking for? Something cute? Something pretty? Something *sexy*, perhaps?"

The question flustered Mariana a little, but she quickly regained her composure and thought about what might suit Mira the best.

"Something cute, I think," she said decisively. Mira was cute; ergo, she needed cute underwear.

"I see." Lythalia gave Mariana's body a quick up-and-down glance. "Not particularly adventurous, but it's your first time. And what color?"

"Color?" Mariana muttered. This was a question where she could actually put her feng shui to use. What aspect would best suit Mira's disposition and fortune? "A light green would be best, I think."

Light green, the color of new grass, would improve health and bring stability. Mariana nodded at her choice. The health of Master Danblf's pupil was always paramount, and gods knew the girl needed some stability.

"Light green," Lythalia parroted, then slipped past, catching Mariana's hand to pull the fairy along in her wake. "I can see that. Let's take a quick look."

Soon, Lythalia was rummaging through the shelves like a seasoned pro. After watching her for a few moments, Mariana took a peek at the shelf behind her. Then she turned back to the shelf Lythalia was browsing and puzzled over what the difference was—they seemed almost identical to her, but apparently, there was some subtle difference she was missing.

"I'm glad to have bumped into you. It makes me so happy that you're finally showing an interest in fashion," Lythalia remarked as her hand snaked out to snag a pair of cute light-green panties. The elven woman arched an eyebrow as she looked back at her friend. "And starting with underwear instead of clothes? I can't wait to see where this goes!"

Mariana's eyes went wide. "Oh, but this isn't for me, it's—"

She was cut off as Lythalia forced six pairs of panties with matching camisoles into her hands. "For your first time, I'd recommend these!"

"No, but I—"

"They'll look great on you. Look, the changing room is over here. Let's go try them on."

Protests ignored and overwhelmed by her sense of duty to improve her friend's undergarment situation, Lythalia grasped the fairy by the shoulders and marched her to the fitting room. Before she could say anything further, Mariana heard the curtain slide closed behind her.

Alone, she let out a sigh...but as she saw herself reflected in the mirror, she reconsidered. Mira's physique was almost the same as her own, so perhaps there was a silver lining to this mix-up.

Taking off her clothes and putting them on a shelf, she gazed at herself in the large, full-length mirror. The hem of her slip rode across her upper thighs and her drawers just peeked out from underneath. It was what she'd always worn, and she wasn't really interested in reinventing her brand.

Running her hands along the hem of her slip, she gently pulled it off and picked up the camisole. A few moments later, she was sliding the new panties over her hips to complete the ensemble.

"What do you think?" Mariana peeked through a crack in the curtain, but Lythalia whipped the curtain back so she could get the full picture.

"You look spectacular! Better than I imagined!"

Mariana's body was modest but pleasantly proportioned. Her sapphire hair hung softly around her shoulders, and the light-green underwear gently hugged the contours of her pale skin.

"Th-this is kind of embarrassing!" Mariana squeaked before tugging the curtain back to protect herself from the gaze of other customers.

"All right, now try on the others!" Lythalia commanded.

A diamond in the rough. Lythalia had always known there was potential buried in Mariana, but she was surprised at the difference just one pair of underwear had made. She smirked and tried to suppress her excitement for future makeovers and fashion outings with her friend.

Behind the curtain, Mariana looked at herself in the mirror once more.

"It doesn't suit me," she muttered.

"That's not true! Mariana, you are beautiful!" Lythalia said, peeking her head inside the curtain. "And a beautiful girl deserves beautiful clothes."

The statement warmed Mariana's heart, but only for a moment. "But I..."

Taking this matter into her own hands before Mariana chickened out and turned back from the path of fashion, Lythalia burst into the fitting room and closed the curtain behind her. As she made a point-by-point commentary on just how attractive Mariana was, she helped her friend dress in the different underclothes—some sleek, some frilly with ribbons and lace.

Feeling somewhat like a dress-up doll, Mariana listened to what Lythalia was saying as though it were a dream. She fantasized about being just a little bit taller.

"Thank you for helping me find these," Mariana said with a bow after the pair had checked out. All six of Lythalia's suggestions were tucked neatly into her bag.

"Whenever you want to do it again, just let me know! I'll always be glad to help."

Lythalia still had no idea the underwear was for Mira, but Mariana was happy to let it be a misunderstanding. Instead, she gave a little nod and bid her friend a good afternoon.

After parting ways in front of the store, Mariana found a bench in the small nearby plaza and sat down with a tired little sigh. The plaza was crowded with tourists and stalls, and you could see all nine of the Linked Silver Towers from here. All about her, people looked up and marveled at the sight.

As she sat, she gazed blankly at the Tower of Evocation and thought of panties.

Maybe by mixing and matching colors, I can fine-tune my fate.

With feng shui in play, lingerie was suddenly a more interesting field than she'd expected. She'd discovered a new aspect of herself—one that included cute underwear.

Master Danblf... What would he think if he saw them? Would he think they were...cute?

In her mind's eye, the figure of Master Danblf superimposed itself over the Tower of Evocation. Suddenly, her face went even redder than it had been in the fitting room, and she tugged at a lock of hair that fell over her shoulder. Perhaps her interest in underwear went beyond simple feng shui.

As Mariana writhed in embarrassment, she heard something creeping up beside her. She spun toward the presence and found only her shopping bag, but for some reason, it was jostling and shaking. With trepidation, she reached toward the rustling bag, wondering if this was common behavior for modern lingerie.

But just as her hand touched the handle, a cat poked its head out, something small stuck in its mouth—a pair of her new panties.

Their eyes met, and after a brief standoff, the cat growled and took off like a bolt of lightning.

"Oh, kitty, please give that back!" Jumping to her feet, she grabbed her shopping bag and darted off after the cat onto a side street.

Unlike the main street, the side streets were narrow and packed with smaller shops that served the locals more than the tourists. Tools, arms and armor, food vendors—each shop had its own particular offering, but all of them catered to adventurers and craftsmen.

This was the cat's home turf, and it raced along the street, dodging Mariana's grasp as it scampered through stalls and back alleys.

Mariana realized she couldn't keep up on foot. She spread her wings and gently took flight on the ambient currents of mana. As she was a fairy, her wings were delicate things never meant to be aerodynamically sound; rather, she could glide on the air's ambient magic and turn quickly to match the cat's every move.

Flying slightly below the rooftops to keep sight of the cat while avoiding pedestrians and stalls, she quickly got within range of her target. With a swoop, she reached for the felonious feline.

"Ah!"

It abruptly changed directions, as if sensing her apprehensive attempt. It plunged into a narrow gap between buildings that was too small for Mariana to squeeze through.

"Please don't run, kitty!" she called as she peeked into the crevice. The cat didn't reply, but it did keep running to the street on the other side.

With an indignant huff, Mariana spread her wings and took flight again just as a man emerged from a nearby store.

"Miss Mariana? Is something the matter?" he asked in surprise, bags dangling from both hands. He wore robes embellished with a special mark labeling him as one of the few researchers from the Tower of Evocation.

"Can't talk now. A cat just took my underwear," she blurted out before taking off in a hurry.

Her explanation was short and lacking, but the researchers who worked within the Silver Towers were the best of the best when it came to discerning the truth from even the smallest bit of information. His mind set to work at once to solve the problem based on the clues available.

The subject: Mariana's underwear.

The situation: Taken by a cat. In other words, stolen.

But what was particularly important was the item of underwear. He began with a clear picture of Mariana within his mind. Then, using skill that only a true master could attain, he removed clothes from the imaginary Mariana piece by piece until he hit the end of the line.

She wasn't busty enough to need a brassiere, which left only one thing to be stolen.

If a cat had stolen her underwear, that meant Miss Mariana wasn't wearing any—

Realizing what this all must mean, the researcher cast aside the bags and ran off in pursuit.

He never considered how the panties someone was wearing could be stolen right off them. But the moment Mariana had said the word "underwear," all rationality had flown out the window.

Meanwhile, the cat scampered from back alley to side street, exhibiting masterful footwork and leading Mariana on a merry chase. Somehow, she managed to keep sight of it.

At the end of a narrow path was a bench, upon which sat two elderly gentlemen chatting with each other. Both were well-built for their age and bore the scars of old battles across their arms and faces like medals. A cat ran briskly by the pair, followed soon after by a fairy wearing a maid's uniform.

"Wasn't that Miss Mariana? The way she's chasing after that cat reminds me of Mistress Kagura," one of the two said, staring off after the pair and chuckling.

"What are you talking about? Mistress Kagura was always chasing thunder beasts. They look like cats, but they're not the same."

"In all fairness, I think she used to chase thunder beasts *because* they look like cats. Just loved cats, that woman did. Damnedest thing—we were fighting a cat-type monster once and she switched sides and fought with the enemy."

As the two veterans sat reminiscing about days gone by, a large group of men hustled past.

"Now, that there reminded me of the chase for Mistress Artesia."

"You know, me too."

A cry went up from the group as they hurried off. They were clearly driven by animal desire, which added to the uncanny resemblance.

"Did you know she was a widow? She was calm, caring, and gentle. Men would follow her to hell and back if she asked."

"You don't have to tell me. Mistress Artesia couldn't fight to save her own life, being a cleric and all—but she could bless the devil out of her troops! Never had a shortage of fighters willing to swing a sword on her behalf."

The old men sat and remembered bloody battlefields where the fight had been carried by morale and adoration for the Mistress of the Tower of the Holy.

"It's a beautiful day, isn't it?"

The pair looked up at the blue skies and the tranquility set their spirits at ease.

Meanwhile, Mariana finally cornered the cat at the end of an alleyway. With one running and one flying, the only escape for the cat would be in climbing the wall, but Mariana's flight gave her the edge. The cat watched warily and waited for a chance to slip around her side.

"All right, kitty. Time to give it back," she said as she moved in closer, but the cat growled and maintained its distance. It was a standoff.

"Oh, right!" With a sudden flash of inspiration, Mariana pulled a small bag from her skirt pocket and emptied it into her palm. "Hey, kitty, how about a trade?"

In her hand were two cookies—plain and sugar-free. She'd made them that morning to carry as the day's lucky item. She slowly advanced, hand outstretched, and the cat's nose twitched.

Lured in by the scent, the cat tossed aside the neatly folded panties in its mouth and pounced upon the cookies. It must have been hungry because it ravenously tore into the snacks. Mariana gave the cat a gentle pat, then dropped the treats on the ground and backed away. Quietly, she crept around the munching animal and reclaimed her wayward undergarment.

"Well, then, time to head home, I suppose," she muttered and sighed in exhaustion. Glancing at the cat, she fluttered into the sky and headed back toward the Tower of Evocation.

Below, the group of men who'd heard that a cat had stolen her panties rushed into the alleyway.

The tower researcher leading the group looked between the cat, who was absorbed in eating the cookies, and Mariana flying away and instantly grasped the situation. The cat had given away the treasure in exchange for the treat.

But upon closer inspection, this was no ordinary cat. The cat who had been Mariana's adversary for the day was famous among the citizenry of Silverhorn. Known as Tenok, the Heavenly Hunter, his hunting grounds were the plazas about the city where he preyed upon souvenirs of tourists who had stopped to gawk at the towers.

His aim was to snag snacks and other morsels from shopping bags, but in a pinch, any item would do.

To the men, this heist must have been the cat's greatest achievement—for this was the time that Tenok stole Mariana's panties. The accomplishment quickly became legend, and he was admired and revered for act of sheer moxie. Men across the city began to make offerings to Tenok, no doubt reducing the damage done to tourists' souvenir purchases.

But soon, another anomalous occurrence arose.

Cats began flipping girls' skirts. Testimony from one victim stated that she'd been looking at the Silver Towers when Tenok jumped up and pulled at her skirt—and at the same time, a chill ran up her spine, as though someone was staring at her from afar.

What mystery lurks in the Sacred City of Silverhorn?

The culprit may be closer than you think.

AFTERWORD

I DIDN'T DO ONE IN Volume One, but it looks like we're doing an afterword here in Volume Two. My editor gave me free rein to write about whatever I wanted, but I'm still deciding what that might be.

Give me a moment.

I've got an idea. Why not talk about the video games I like? They've somewhat influenced my work, so it's not entirely off-topic.

I can imagine you've already guessed my favorite genre is RPGs. Anything by Square Enix or from the *Tales* series was sure to be amazing, and I rather liked the *Wild Arms* series as well. So many hours of sleep lost. I was so young.

But I always stayed away from RPGs like the *Persona* series that had a more realistic setting.

Then, something happened—I lost interest. Before, when a new *Tales* game was announced, I'd instantly preorder and then sit around waiting and counting the days for the game to launch. Nowadays, I see articles online about new games and I just skip over them.

Some new RPG is announced, and the world goes gaga, and I don't care in the slightest. As someone who loved RPGs, I never thought this would happen to me.

But there are still games that I get hooked on. Games like *Dark Souls* and *The Elder Scrolls* series. Great fantasy games. Though *Dark Souls* might be a bit too dark at times.

The Elder Scrolls has an MMO now too, it seems. But it doesn't have a Japanese client (as of September 2012), so it seems a bit daunting for someone with only around a middle-school–level grasp of English. But I won't let that stop me! Maybe, even if it is just in English...I'm still thinking about it.

Anyway, the game I'm most interested in at the moment is probably... Hey, don't act so uninterested!

If you're taking the time to read this, then you have no one to blame but yourself!

It's called *Deep Down*. As soon as I saw the trailer, I was hooked.

But, you know...work. I won't be able to play the game; I have to keep writing. But I can dream, can't I? Dreaming about the future, when I have the money and the time...

Oh, right, speaking of dreams, this summer (2014), Universal Studios Japan finally launched it! You know, that thing they've been showing all over TV!

That's right! The Wizarding World of Harry Potter!

I wonder how many of you who are still bothering to read this have already been? I'm so jealous.

I'd rather spend a day in there than at any other attraction. As someone who loves fantasy, that's my dream. I would love to live there. It's sure to stir the imagination. Maybe spark a few story ideas. Or perhaps that's just the writer in me talking.

Right now, going there is my number one goal. And then buying all the merchandise. I have to at least get myself a wand! And cast a spell. I want a robe too. Preferably all four. This dream is growing. Oh, well, it's still a ways off.

I might have to win the lottery. I have to buy a ticket first, though.

Oh, well, escapism is one of my hobbies, alongside enjoying fine art. I'll get lost looking at the fantastic and nostalgic images I've collected along the way and imagine what it would be like to visit or live in such places.

Did you look at the cover? Just like Volume One, it was drawn by fuzichoco!

I love fuzichoco's illustrations. They're so full of charm, it's like they've captured a scene from a world and you can almost make out the other parts of the world that weren't drawn.

My imagination is soaring.

Since I'm just a humble writer, I meander in my short sleeves into that world looking for inspiration. As I wander this great world asking for booksellers to let me leave my book somewhere in their store, the inviting tones of a festival greet me. Then I leap onto a train with no fixed destination. From a high place, I watch the sunset paint the city in colors.

Ahh, I wish I were there.

I'd like to take this moment to thank fuzichoco from the

bottom of my heart, for showing me those amazing worlds and for drawing the covers and internal illustrations.

fuzichoco, thank you so very much! Thank you for your continued support!

And finally...

Thank you all for purchasing this book. Thanks to you, I keep getting closer to that goal. You keep helping me get closer to USJ, where fantasy is made reality.

I'll see you next time.

CREATOR PROFILES

RYUSEN HIROTSUGU

Still suffering from childhood delusions. A fairy doctor said the case is terminal and there's nothing that can be done. Nevertheless, he isn't pessimistic and lives each day to the fullest. Even if he vanishes, he just hopes that he'll be remembered.

FUZICHOCO

An illustrator who was born in Chiba and now lives in Tokyo. Draws all sorts of things, but primarily works on books and card games. Lives on chocolate.